Flurry the Bear

The Throne of Frost

J.S. Skye

Flurry the Bear

The Throne of Frost

2nd Edition – January 2015
First Published – July 2013

The Throne of Frost
(Flurry the Bear – Book 3)
Copyright © 2015 J.S. Skye
All rights reserved.
www.FlurryTheBear.com

Cover art by Luís Figueiredo, Francois Beauregard,
J.S. Skye, & Tony Washington

ISBN: 0692372547
ISBN-13: 978-0692372548

CONTENTS

CHAPTER 1
THE JOURNEY HOME

A beautiful new day fast approached. The sky radiated its sapphire hue from horizon-to-horizon. Not a single cloud broke its vibrant color. The sun advanced along its circuit to cast its beams down through the vastly forested landscape. The heavenly feel of the dawn was challenged only by the cheer and laughter which echoed throughout the far-off reaches of the timber.

A well-armed company of feline warriors marched with a purpose. The detachment of cats accompanied three small ponies and their riders. These three passengers were the source of the great laughter that resonated throughout the wooded landscape.

On the back of the lead pony sat an adorable teddy bear cub with pure white fur that matched the color of his pony. He wore only a blue scarf with two little snowflakes embroidered at one end.

The cub added to the merriment. He giggled and laughed along with his sister Fall, and his friend Caboose. "Okay, I have one for you," the bear cub addressed to his sister. "Why should you never tell secrets to a coffee maker?"

Fall giggled. She looked especially cute in her blue dress. She had two blue bows, one above each ear, which matched the rest of her apparel. She giggled again and replied,

"I don't know. Why?"

"Because it might spill the beans," answered her brother.

They both cackled together. "Oh, Flurry! You're so silly!" Fall shook her head at her brother. "Okay. I have another one for you," she enthusiastically added. "What do cows do for fun?"

Flurry thought about it for a moment before he responded. "I don't know. What?"

"They watch moo-vies. Get it? Moo-vies."

Flurry clutched his belly and bellowed loudly. He laughed so hard that he tumbled off of his pony. The accident only made them laugh all the more.

The cream-colored polar bear, Caboose, was Flurry's most loyal companion. He, unfortunately, did not understand any of their jokes and riddles, but he laughed right along with them just the same. However, even he appreciated Flurry's fall. Caboose laughed heartily at the cub's blunder.

The three bears sustained their amusement until it was interrupted by one of their cat guardians. The Tikalico warriors kept watch over the cubs to ensure their safe passage through the vast and dangerous land. "We're approaching the territory of Mezarim. We should be arriving at Ursus soon."

"Yay!" Fall broke from her continued amusement at her brother's blunder to exclaim.

Flurry did not share in her excitement anymore. In fact, Flurry's countenance drastically changed.

"What's wrong?" his sister inquired.

"Oh, nothing," Flurry replied. He focused his gaze on the ground and kicked at the dirt. He was not a good liar, and Fall had quickly learned how to read her brother's emotions since she first met him only a matter of days prior.

"Come on, Flurry! You aren't fooling me! What is it?"

"I don't want to talk about it!" he sharply lashed back.

"You can tell me. We're family."

"I said I don't want to talk about it!"

Taken aback by Flurry's sudden mood swing, Fall crossed her arms and turned away from him. "Fine! Have it your way!"

Flurry was helped back up onto the pony by one of the guards, but his reluctance to cooperate was apparent. Flurry moved as slowly as he possibly could. He knew that trouble drew near. In the excitement of his previous adventure, he had lost all track of time and had completely forgotten about the circumstances of how that adventure began.

Flurry was reminded that the last thing he had done, prior to his journey down to the land of the Sourpie, was throw a fit and sneak out of his parents' house. He had run off to a distant land without informing anyone – not even his friends knew what had happened to him.

Flurry cringed when he imagined how sternly he would be disciplined by his parents in Ursus, and then once more by his adopted family when he got back to Middleasia. Flurry had been told that disciplinary correction was a form of love, but that did not mean he had to like it.

Flurry had been bad, and he knew that he

deserved the corrective action he would receive upon their arrival at the North Pole. "Excuse me! Excuse me! Mr. Cat! Is there a chance that we could go a bit slower, please?"

"Slower?" Fall interjected.

"Yeah! You know, so we can take in the sights more," Flurry responded.

"Oh, now I see! You're afraid that Mama and Papa are going to scold you for running away, aren't you?"

"No."

"Yes, you are!"

"No, I'm not!"

"Yes, you are!"

"No, I'm not!"

Before their argument could turn into a shouting match, Flurry turned away and looked back at the turf. The cub had a sinking feeling in his chest with each step his pony took toward his inevitable doom. Tears formed in his eyes, but he quickly wiped them away so that his sister would not see them.

"Flurry, maybe they'll go easy on you since you not only saved the lives of others, but you also united the Sourpie with their brothers and sisters in Tikalico. Not to mention that you stopped Isangrim! Maybe Mr. Kringle will stick up for you," Fall tried to comfort her brother.

"It's no use. Mama and Papa are going to be so angry at me. I'm going to be grounded for the rest of my life." Flurry's eyes watered.

At that moment, Caboose rode up next to him and said, "Sare, sare." That was his way of saying "There, there," but he always pronounced words that contained a "th" as if they were an "s" instead. Caboose did not know what else to do or say, but he wanted to comfort his best friend.

Flurry continued to be downcast. As they approached the edge of the forest, they beheld patches of snow spread sporadically out ahead of them. The further they went, the more the landscape changed from green to white and the beautiful blue sky became gray and overcast. It was like the weather had matched Flurry's gloomy thoughts.

A fog formed. Visibility was low, but Flurry knew they were near home, because he could smell the delicious aroma of bread from the town's bakery. Before long, Flurry beheld the golden glow of shop window lights through the fog. When their entire caravan had reached the town center, Flurry noticed Christopher Kringle and most of the teddy bear village were present. They stood by and waited for the arrival of the three cubs on their ponies.

The horses came to a stop, and Flurry watched in horror as the cat warriors from Tikalico spoke with Christopher. Before Flurry had a chance to scan the crowd, Fall had already located their family members.

"Mama! Papa!" Fall shouted. She jumped down from her mount and rushed over to them. Tears streamed down their faces as they embraced their daughter.

Flurry cried, and buried his face in the pony's pearly-white mane. Caboose hopped down, went over to Flurry, and gazed up at him. "Go away, Caboose! I'm just going to pretend that I'm part of the horsey. We have the same fur color, so maybe I'll be lucky and nobody will notice me here."

Caboose took hold of Flurry's foot and tugged. His intent was to coerce Flurry to get down. However, Caboose pulled too hard and caused Flurry to topple from the pony and down onto Caboose.

"Sorry," Caboose said.

"That's okay. Thanks for breaking my fall at least," Flurry replied.

"You're welcome!"

Flurry stood up and brushed the snow from himself and then off of Caboose. When Flurry looked up from his minor fumble, his mama and papa stood there next to his pony. Tears trickled down their cheeks.

"Before you yell at me, I can ex ..." Flurry's statement was cut short when his mother and father grabbed him and held him close. Both of them cried and hugged their boy tightly.

Flurry's mother was the first to speak. "Son, we missed you so much!"

Flurry was perplexed and asked, "You aren't mad at me?"

"Of course we are," his mother answered and wiped some of her tears away. "But your correction can wait for later. We just want to hold you for now. We were worried sick about you and your sister. We thought we had lost you both." The entire Snow family cried and hugged each other further.

Flurry felt comforted. He knew he was in trouble, but he no longer worried about his punishment. He was happy to know that he was still deeply loved and missed by his parents. He realized he had been wrong in his assumption that his parents had replaced him with Fall, or that they no longer loved him. Flurry felt such relief to be home and safe in the arms of his loving family again.

While they held each other, Christopher approached. "Flurry, is this true?" he asked.

"Uh, oh!" Flurry shouted and jumped back a few steps. He put his arms behind his back, looked up, and replied, "Caboose did it!"

Christopher chuckled, "Yes, Caboose did do it. All three of you did it. I'm proud to know that the cats from Tikalico have now been reunited with their brothers and sisters from Agrio. Thanks to you, an age-old feud has ended, and the two kings stand together again. You even managed to throw a wrench in Isangrim's tyranny. You're to be commended for this. I don't condone what you've put your friends and family through, but I'm proud that you showed integrity and courage to do what was right when in the face of danger and impossible odds. There will be a dinner banquet tonight at my home to honor our guests from Tikalico. Everyone's invited. Tomorrow, you and I will have a little chat about your recent behavior."

Christopher turned to the crowd and announced the reception. The town cheered. Many of the bears rushed off to make early preparations. Christopher led the cat warriors away with him, along a cobblestone path which led out of the village. Flurry, his friends, and family were all that remained.

Flurry wiped away his tears and looked over at Caboose and the rest of his friends that stood by his side. They had accompanied him to Ursus nearly two weeks prior, and also had been worried about

Flurry and his companions.

Flurry ran up and hugged Noah, the tall, slender lion who stood beside Caboose. He was Flurry's best friend. Noah was deeply pleased to see that Flurry was safe and sound.

Their adopted mother in Middleasia had tasked the lion with the duty of protecting and watching over Flurry. Due to that charge, it was such a relief that Flurry was back unharmed. Noah had no idea how he would ever be able to face their mother again if anything bad happened to Flurry.

In fact, Noah had secretly made a vow in his heart that, from now on, he would be ever vigilant. He would make sure Flurry and the others were safe.

Noah was the most mature and dependable of the bunch. It was his duty to look after them, but he had been at the dinner table with the Snow family on the morning of the entire incident. He frequently replayed the event in his head. The poor lion constantly criticized himself for being at the dining table. Noah did not have a mouth, and therefore had no need for or the means to eat food. He should have been at Flurry's side. At least that is what Noah believed he should have done that day.

Flurry gave the other lion, named Boaz, a hug, but he had to get down on one knee for that. Boaz was very small, unlike his lanky brother Noah. Boaz often wore glasses and his mane was so bushy that you could not see his ears.

Last, but not least, Flurry reached out and patted Honja on the head. The little brown rabbit was normally grumpy around Flurry.

However, this day he was pleased to see Flurry, too. He allowed Flurry to pat him on the head just this once. If this had been any other day, Honja would have been angered by this action. He did not like to be touched, and he especially hated being patted on the head. Flurry always forgot about this fact and would do it anyway, but this day Honja was kind enough to let it slide. As much as Flurry frustrated Honja, he too had been worried and was now happy to have the bear cub back.

After everyone had hugged, shed their tears, and spent time reuniting, they followed Mr. and Mrs. Snow back to their family's abode.

The rest of the day was pleasant despite the fact that Flurry was lectured, just as he knew he would be. His parents informed him of how precious he was, and how much they loved him before they explained why they were also very angry at him for being irresponsible and selfish. Flurry had endangered both his and his sister's life while he simultaneously made everyone in Ursus worry about them.

Flurry apologized, and it was understood that his adopted family would also be informed of an adequate disciplinary action.

Despite having been reprimanded, the rest of the day was great. Flurry spent most of the time outside. The cubs made snowbears, played tag, and went sledding. Flurry's sister instigated a snowball fight that became the highlight of their day. All of the young ones were happy. They giggled and laughed the day away, while Mr. and Mrs. Snow watched from the front window of their home.

The evening came quickly, and Flurry could not believe it was time for the banquet in honor of the Tikalico warriors. The cubs were all immensely excited about the banquet. In fact, Flurry's mouth already watered at the thought of all of the delicious food that would be there. Even better was the possibility of the tasty treats he could have for dessert.

The cubs were gathered by the door when a chill came over Flurry. The North Pole had always been cold, but not cold enough that it would require any of them to wear warmer clothes. It had always been a tolerable level of cold.

Mr. and Mrs. Snow opened the door and immediately noticed the sudden temperature drop. "That's strange," Mr. Snow commented. "It hasn't been this cold in my lifetime. It has always been relatively pleasant in this part of Mezarim."

His words did not reach the cubs in time. They were excited to see snow fall from above. The flakes glistened in the sunlight so much so that it caught Fall's attention. She hastily rushed out the front door. "Wow! Look! It's snowing!" she shouted and spun around with her arms in the air, but she quickly ran back into the house when the frigid air disturbed her. "It's so cold!" she exclaimed to the other younglings.

"Indeed!" her father replied. "Everyone come here! Put on these winter coats. I keep extras here just in case of a winter storm." Mr. Snow opened a chest that sat near the front door and pulled out a variety of winter coats, pants, and boots for Flurry and company. They bundled up as quickly as they could – after all, they did not want to miss a single moment of the banquet dinner.

"Papa, why is it so cold?" Flurry asked. The cub looked up at his father and continued. "I don't remember it ever being this cold before."

"I'm not sure, Son, but it can't be good. There might be a bad storm coming." Mr. Snow answered while he scanned the sky. He pulled his hood up over his head and stepped out the door. Mr. Snow had a bad feeling about it, but the weather would have to wait since they were expected at Christopher's home.

Flurry was the last to bundle up. The cold had never bothered him before and certainly did not now. He reluctantly grabbed a coat. It had fur around the hem of the hood. Flurry zipped up the coat, pulled the fuzzy hood over his head, and ran outside to join his friends. Mrs. Snow closed the door after them and followed everyone down the path.

Flurry skipped the entire way, though he would momentarily pause from time-to-time to pick up some snow and throw it at someone. Their trip might have been quicker had they not been interrupted by a few snowball fights along the way.

What would have been a pleasant journey turned out to be bitter as the temperature continued to drop. The wind picked up, and the clouds obscured the light from the sun. The snow fell more heavily. Thankfully, they reached Christopher Kringle's house. Flurry gazed at the beautiful stone and recalled how he had always thought of it as a castle.

With a knock at the door, they were greeted by Catherine and her wolf, Vallidore. Flurry loved her wolf dearly. The bear cub liked to cuddle with the wolf and pet him every chance he got. However, Flurry had a hard time with the wolf's name, so he resorted to calling him Doggy.

When the door opened, Flurry exclaimed, "Doggy!" and ran up to the wolf and hugged his leg. Everyone chuckled when they saw how affectionate Flurry was toward Mrs. Kringle's companion.

This wolf was no ordinary wolf. Firstly, he was much larger than a typical wolf. His back stood higher than Catherine's waistline. Instead of yellow eyes, he had blue, and his fur was just as white as Flurry's. The wolf bore various markings upon his fur. The decorative markings were writings in the ancient Polarin language. Very few could read or understand the beautiful script on the wolf's fur.

"Okay, Vallidore, step back and let our guests in," Catherine instructed her wolf. He was very protective of the Kringle couple, and was devoted to them.

Catherine Kringle was very lovely. She stood tall and had a slender frame. Her head was adorned with long, fiery-red hair which flowed down to the middle of her back. Even at her age, she had managed to retain much of her youthful beauty. Christopher was very proud of her, and he loved her very much.

The entourage of plush visitors entered the house. Songs, laughter, and cheer could be heard from within. "Come! Everyone is gathering in the main hall." Catherine informed her guests and led them through a set of double-doors into a large, spacious room where the festivities took place. Flurry's face lit up with delight at the sight of the abundant array of cuisine. He licked his lips and ran off toward one of the tables of food.

"Flurry, wait for me!" Fall shouted while in hot pursuit of her brother.

Flurry's other plush companions also ran toward the food. However, Noah stood fast and watched Flurry like a hawk. He was not about to let any harm come to his friend, and the only way to ensure Flurry's safety was to keep an eye on him at all times. Noah had no need for food, so it was not necessary for him to be with the rest of his brothers at the dinner table.

"You aren't joining your friends?" asked

Mr. Snow. He looked down at Noah with a surprised face. The lion cub may not have been able to speak, but he was able to communicate very well. He pointed at Flurry, made the shape of binoculars around his eyes, and then stood up straight and saluted. Mr. Snow smiled when he realized what Noah had told him. "Well, thank you, Noah. I appreciate you watching out for my son. Carry on." Mr. Snow saluted the lion before he turned to his wife and escorted her to their table of choice.

By this point, Flurry had already gotten himself situated at his bench with a pile of food heaped up on his plate. He felt like he had died and gone to Heaven. Flurry stuffed himself with so many delicious choices of culinary delights. However, the cub made sure to leave room for dessert.

Dessert was certainly Flurry's favorite part of the meal, and he especially loved Mrs. Kringle's chocolate chip cookies and hot chocolate. He had not had them for more than three months, back when Flurry still lived in Ursus. In Middleasia, Flurry's human mother often made him chocolate milk or chocolate cake, but Mrs. Kringle still made the best cookies.

The night was full of fun and laughter. Flurry's escorts from Tikalico were treated like royalty and entertained for hours. Food was abundant, and Flurry felt at home and content.

Meanwhile, as everyone inside kept warm, a storm brewed outside the walls of the Kringle house. The wind grew stronger, and the temperature dropped sharply. It was unlike anything anyone in Ursus had ever experienced before.

Unfortunately, this weather pattern was familiar to Christopher, and it troubled him deeply. He recalled the last time there was such an icy blizzard. It was during an age when Jack Frost ruled.

CHAPTER 2
DRIZZLE'S CONFLICT

The next morning came, but the sun did not shine as it was accustomed to. This day brought another cloudy sky, ruled by strong wind and frosty conditions. The snow had let up temporarily, but the previous night of blizzard-like weather left a deep blanket of snow and ice on everything.

Despite the harshness outside, the teddy bear cubs and the cats from Tikalico were nice and warm within the walls of Christopher Kringle's home. The adult bears had gone back to their own houses for the night, but the cubs had all begged for permission to stay with the Kringles, and their pleas had been granted.

Most of the cubs slept in bunk beds in one of the many rooms of the house. Some of the cubs slept under blankets upon various pieces of furniture or nestled up by the fireplace. Flurry, however, slept cuddled next to Vallidore.

Flurry sat up from his slumber when he heard the sound of the breakfast bell. Vallidore got up and walked off, which left Flurry without his warm, furry friend to snuggle.

Flurry stretched out his arms and yawned. He got up and looked around, but found most of the other cubs still asleep. Flurry followed the smell of food into another room where Christopher dined with the Tikalico warriors. From the look of things, they had just finished up. "It appears you have a visitor," the red-haired beauty whispered to her husband.

Christopher chortled, looked down, and saw Flurry gazing up at him. "Well, hello there, little one. You're certainly up early."

"Hello, Santa! Yeah, I know. What are you doing?" Flurry yawned and rubbed his eyes.

"We had an early meal so these fine fellows can be on their way back home. It's a long journey, and Catherine wanted to be sure they were well fed first," Christopher informed the inquisitive cub.

"Is there any food left for me?"

The jolly man chuckled again. "I'm certain that my dear can make you something. What would you like?"

"P'sghetti?" Flurry's eyes widened. He put his paws together, as if he were begging, and licked his lips.

The Kringle couple and the cats laughed in unison at Flurry's request.

"Certainly! I believe we have spaghetti somewhere," Christopher answered.

"Yay!" Flurry shouted. Catherine smiled and opened the cupboard to get out some pasta.

The smell of food eventually woke the other cubs up, one-by-one. Before long, everyone was awake and wanted food of their own. Catherine now had her work cut out for her, but she did not mind. In fact, she loved to cook, and derived great joy from the smiles that she put upon the faces of others with her food. Her culinary skills began as a hobby, but were now a passion. Thankfully, she had servants to help her when it became too much for one person to handle alone.

After a hearty breakfast, some of the cubs tried to go outside to play, but they quickly rushed back indoors. "It's so cold!" shouted Flurry's cousin, Bliz.

"Maybe we could all play inside," Fall suggested.

"Great idea!" Bliz answered. Bliz was a good friend to Flurry and Fall in addition to being their cousin. He was the middle child of three, the son of Chip and Bubbles. He was very small, and his fur was pure white, just like Flurry's. On his head he wore a little red cap that came to a point with a white fluffy ball at the end. Bliz was very hyperactive and often spoke so fast that it was difficult to understand what he had said.

Flurry's school friend, Sunny, joined the rest of Flurry's friends in a game of hide-and-seek. While they played together, another little bear wanted to join in. This little bear looked almost identical to Flurry except that his fur was the color of charcoal, and he had a crimson-colored scarf with storm clouds stitched at the bottom near the tassels.

The cub's name was Drizzle. He was a member of the Rain family. The Snow family and the Rain family were both very prominent families in Ursus.

Despite Drizzle's adorable features, he was often discouraged. He frequently was excluded and felt unwanted by others. Drizzle's parents were continually displeased with him. No matter how hard he worked nor what he did to make them proud, they were consistently unmoved. In fact, Drizzle's parents harbored a deeply held grudge against Christopher Kringle. Mrs. Rain had wanted a cub of her own for quite some time. The Rain family admired Flurry and wanted their own cub to be just like him. They fashioned their idea of the perfect cub and asked Christopher to give him life.

Christopher granted their request. However, Mr. and Mrs. Rain noticed that Drizzle was not like any of the other cubs. He was very different in numerous ways.

Mr. and Mrs. Rain realized that Drizzle struggled a great deal with social interactions. He found it difficult to fit in with the other cubs. As a result, Drizzle spent most of his free time in his room, drawing or doing something related to mathematics. Numbers became Drizzle's friends, because he could always rely on them to be true and consistent.

In school, Drizzle was the worst student. The cub saw letters backwards when he tried to read, and he had difficulties with some aspects of speech.

Thankfully, Drizzle managed to befriend Flurry's cousin. Bliz liked everyone, no matter what. He did not differentiate between what others considered to be pleasant or unpleasant company. Many found Drizzle to be annoying or tedious to talk to. However, all individuals were created equal in Bliz's sight. Drizzle and Bliz got along well and talked a lot about interests they had in common. They shared a love for things which others considered to be "geeky".

On this cold and blustery day, Drizzle decided to make an attempt to befriend Flurry once again. Over the years, Flurry and Drizzle had not gotten along, and their interactions often left either of them angry or in tears. *Today will be different,* Drizzle thought to himself. "Hey guys!" the black-furred bear bellowed and waved to the other cubs.

"Hey, Drizzle!" Bliz enthusiastically answered back. He waved so fast that his arm was but a blur.

"What do you want?" Flurry asked with contempt in his voice. He peeked his head out of a gift-wrapped box at the sound of Drizzle's greeting. The lid rested on top of Flurry's head as he spoke. "Can't you see we're playing here? Go away!" Flurry's tone was as cold and uninviting as the weather outside.

"Flurry! Shame on you! Don't be like that!" Fall scolded her brother. She crawled out from under the couch to greet the newcomer. She approached Drizzle and tried to mend the situation. "Don't mind my brother, he can be rude sometimes." As Fall spoke, Drizzle blushed and redirected his sight down toward the floor. "Here, let me introduce you to my new friends from Middleasia," Fall continued. "The tall lion standing behind you is Noah." Noah waved. "The smaller lion is Boaz."

"Howdy!" Boaz replied from behind a curtain.

"I'm not sure where Caboose is," Fall continued. "And the cute little rabbit hiding behind that potted plant is Honja."

Honja peeked out at Fall and gave her an angry glare. He felt outraged that his position had been compromised, and that he would have to find a new hiding spot. Drizzle walked over to the pot and was about to pat Honja on the head when Fall halted him – just in time. "Stop! Don't pat him on the head! He hates that!"

"Oh, sorry!" Drizzle replied. It was a good thing that she warned him. Honja had a look of horror on his face when he saw Drizzle's paw reach out toward his head. In fact, he was so terrified that he dropped the lollipop he had been licking and became as still as stone.

While Fall introduced her friends, Flurry had come out from hiding and joined the others. "He can't play with us!" Flurry insisted.

"Why not?" Fall asked.

"Just because."

"That's not a good enough reason!" Fall shot back at her immature sibling.

"He's mean!" Flurry insisted.

"No, I'm not! You're mean!" Drizzle spoke up in his own defense.

"Oh, yeah? Well, why do you make fun of me for not having a tail?"

"Because you and Sunny make fun of me every day! You say that I'm dumb, and a weirdo!"

"Well, maybe if you didn't act so strange, we wouldn't have a reason to laugh at you," Sunny interjected. The yellow-furred teddy bear had been there all along, but had kept quiet up until now.

Sunny mocked Drizzle. In an altered voice he said, "Ouch! That light is too bright! Oh, my head hurts from all of the noise!" Sunny giggled and pointed at Drizzle.

Whether it was Sunny's comment or the fact that he wore a red handkerchief around his neck, the rest of the cubs perceived him as an outlaw. They glared at Sunny. Sunny realized that his actions were wrong, but he grinned anyway.

Drizzle cried and ran off. Flurry felt bad for what had just transpired. He did not condone Sunny's comments, but Sunny was his friend and he was prone to take Sunny's side over Drizzle's.

"Flurry! You and Sunny are acting so childish! Can't you two put your differences aside long enough to play a simple game together?" Fall shouted at her brother and Sunny. She turned her gaze to Flurry and

directed her next statement solely to him.
"You clearly didn't learn anything from our
time with the Sourpie!" Fall was enraged at
her brother's pettiness.

Not to be made to look foolish in front of
others; Flurry turned his back to Fall and
crossed his arms. Fall was incensed. "Fine
then! You go back to your game! I'm not
playing anymore!" Fall shouted.

"Fine!" Flurry barked back at her. "Come
on, guys! We don't need her!" Flurry
walked away from Fall in haste, but his
conscience got the better of him. He took
only a few steps, and then turned back. With
a sigh, Flurry relented, "Okay! He can play
with us."

"Good! That's better!" Fall's voice
sounded well pleased, but when she looked
over to invite Drizzle back into the fold, he

was nowhere to be found. "Drizzle? Drizzle?" she called out, but she did not receive a reply.

Fall and Flurry ran over to where they last saw him, but he was not there. "Where could he have gone?" Fall thought out loud. Flurry shrugged.

"I'm sorry," Flurry commented. He looked at the floor in shame. "I shouldn't have been so mean to him."

Fall rubbed Flurry's back to console him. "It's okay. It's in the past now. Let's move forward. I tell you what, you and the others go play. I'll find Drizzle, and bring him back. Okay?"

"Okay," Flurry answered and ran back with the rest of the cubs.

Fall looked all through the house but could not find Drizzle anywhere. She was about to give up her search when she heard the sound of sobbing. Fall climbed up on a chair and looked out one of the windows to behold Drizzle outside in the cold. He shivered and cried as he sat alone. Fall grabbed her coat, and an extra one for Drizzle, before she stepped outside to meet him.

"You know, it's too cold to be out here without a coat," Fall said. Drizzle continued to sob. "What's wrong?" Fall asked and put the coat around him.

Fall stood next to the despondent cub. Eventually, Drizzle decided to speak to her. "I just want to have a friend. I don't know why Flurry doesn't like me. It feels like nobody likes me."

"I like you, and believe me, you're in good company. My brother was not happy when he found out that he had a sister either, but he got over it. It just takes time for Flurry to adjust. He's a bit stubborn, but he has a very kind and caring heart deep down. I hope you'll give him another chance."

Drizzle wiped away his tears and nodded in agreement. He stood up, and the two cubs re-entered the house together. When they returned, the other cubs were no longer playing hide-and-seek. Instead, Flurry was telling stories about his adventure to the cubs. As Flurry continued to brag about his great deeds, Drizzle felt more insecure with each passing moment. Drizzle felt alienated and distant. He thought that he might be able to win the others over if he proved himself on an adventure of his own.

It was this moment when Drizzle remembered the forbidden land of Ursidea.

In school, all of the cubs would dare each other to go there to prove that they were not cowards, but nobody ever went. There were many rumors and legends that surrounded that region. A lot of the cubs claimed that anyone who had the courage to enter the land of Ursidea would never return. Drizzle thought this would be the ideal way to prove his worth and to show that he could be just as brave as Flurry.

With only a moment's hesitation, Drizzle drifted away from the group and made his way to the front door. He grabbed a walking stick and stealthily slipped out of the house. The stick had the words "Path Finder" carved into it. Drizzle took note of where it was propped up against Christopher Kringle's wall, near the door, so that he could return it when he got back.

Though Drizzle opened the door carefully and left quietly, he was not as sly as he thought. Fall glimpsed the little bear as he snuck away.

Fall immediately got up from her seat, put on her coat, and ran for the door. "Where are you going? I'm just getting to the good part," Flurry called out from his crowd of fans.

"Flurry, it's probably because of you that Drizzle has run off again. I'm going to go and bring him back," Fall replied. She ran out and slammed the door behind her. It was clear to everyone that Fall was angry with her brother again. Flurry stood there uncertain of what to do for a moment, but then returned to his storytelling.

Many hours passed, and the parents came to retrieve their cubs. It was close to noon when Mr. Snow arrived at the house all bundled up. "Flurry, gather your things. It's time to go home," Mr. Snow informed his son. He looked around the room and noticed the absence of his daughter. "Where's Fall?" Flurry's father asked.

"I don't know. I'm sure she's around here somewhere," Flurry answered.

Mr. Snow went through the house and looked for Fall, but he was unable to find her. He stopped by Christopher's study and rapped on the door.

"Come on in," the voice behind the door answered.

Mr. Snow entered the study. Christopher sat reclined in a chair with his nose in a book. Vallidore lay on the floor next to the fireplace. "Chris, I'm sorry to bother you, but have you seen my daughter? Flurry and the other cubs do not know where she is."

Christopher immediately sat up in his chair, slapped the book shut, and looked intently at Mr. Snow. "You mean she's not here?"

"No sir, she's not," answered Fall's distressed father.

Christopher looked concerned. He shot up from his chair, tossed the book down, and rushed for the door. He went straight to the main hall where all of the bears had gathered. "Listen up, everyone!" He raised his voice to be heard over the various conversations. "Has anyone seen Fall?"

The guests looked to and fro. Each of them had a confused expression upon their face. "Let me put this another way. Does anyone know where Fall is?"

Flurry stood up to answer. "No, Santa, we

haven't seen her for a while now. Drizzle is gone, too. Fall said she was going to bring him back, because he ran away or something."

Christopher's face had a look of sheer horror. He shot a glance at Vallidore, and the wolf instantly ran out of the room. "This is bad news. If they aren't here, or at home, then they're probably outside, and there's a bad storm on the way."

"Oh no!" shouted the guests.

"As bad as last night's storm?" one of his visitors inquired.

"Worse!" Christopher replied. The bears chattered amongst themselves. The room was tense. Fear gripped most of Christopher's company.

Before long, the man interrupted the chatter and addressed the crowd again.

"Everyone is to stay here until this storm passes. You'll all be safe here. However, I fear that Fall and Drizzle may be in grave danger. I'm looking for a volun …"

Before Christopher could finish his sentence, Vallidore returned, all covered with snow. "What did you find, my friend?" Christopher asked.

To everyone's surprise, the wolf spoke. "There are two sets of tracks leading off to the southwest. If they continue on that path, they'll enter Ursidea."

Everyone gasped and murmured. Christopher raised his hands. "Quiet, please! I need everyone's attention. I don't know the reason or the circumstances behind why Drizzle or Fall would wander off like this, but if we're to ensure their safety, someone needs to go after them. As I was about to say, I'm looking for a volunteer."

Without hesitation, Flurry raised his paw. "I'll go!"

Mr. Snow instantly objected. "Flurry! It's not safe! Fall could be in danger. Your mother and I don't want to risk losing you, too. We only just got you back. Please reconsider and stay here with us, where it's safe," Flurry's father pleaded with his son.

Christopher addressed Vallidore. "If you were to leave now, could you catch up to them before they reach Ursidea?"

"I'll do my best, but with the snow being so deep, it's unlikely. From what I hear, they also have a few hours head start."

The other bears panicked and looked to each other for answers. "Very well. Flurry, you and Vallidore may go to retrieve your sister and Drizzle."

"Wait a minute!" Mr. Snow shouted. His concern was taken into account. Flurry's father's feelings were important to Christopher. However, Christopher had a hunch that Flurry would be needed on this errand, and he wanted to ensure that they all returned safely.

With a worried expression upon his face, Christopher addressed Mr. Snow's concerns. "Unfortunately, if my fears prove to be true, nobody will be safe, not even in my home." The bears all gasped. Expressions of fear and confusion came over their faces. The bears did not know what was going on, and it made them feel insecure.

Christopher continued. "I understand how you feel, but I believe that Flurry is the right one for this journey. He won't be alone. Vallidore will go with him and protect him.

This must be done quickly, or else they'll be caught in the blizzard."

As he spoke, Noah stepped forward and saluted Christopher. The lion walked over and stood next to Flurry. Christopher smiled and said, "Very well, you shall go, too. It's been settled. Noah, Flurry, and Vallidore are to go find them. Please go now and return with haste. May the Great King guide your path!"

When Christopher had finished his blessing, Vallidore bowed to him, helped get Flurry and Noah on his back, and darted out the front door as speedily as possible.

The snow was very deep, and the wind had picked up, but nothing could hold Vallidore back. He trampled the snow beneath his paws at full speed.

Back at Christopher Kringle's house,

there was unrest and concern over what had transpired. Christopher rushed up to his wife and whispered something in her ear. She nodded and bolted out of the room. "What's going on?" the bears asked.

"I'm not entirely certain, but the frigid cold, the incoming snowstorm, and the cubs heading toward Ursidea can't all be just a coincidence. I have a hunch. I hope I'm wrong, but I'm taking precautions just in case." With his final comment, he left the room and closed the double doors behind him.

At that moment, Caboose popped his head out of a wardrobe and shouted, "Here I am!"

Boaz shook his head. "Caboose, we quit playing hide-and-seek hours ago."

"You didn't find me! So I win!" Caboose replied.

CHAPTER 3
THE CAVE AT URSIDEA

The temperature continued to decrease, and the wind grew stronger, but Drizzle was determined and would not be swayed. He had to prove that he, too, was courageous and of value. Drizzle was grateful to have the staff he had brought from Christopher Kringle's house. Without it to anchor him in the snow, the wind might have blown him away.

Drizzle continued to focus his attention on reaching Ursidea. He did not hear the faint voice on the wind which called out his name. "Drizzle! Drizzle! Wait!" Fall shouted out to him. She was quite a distance behind him, but his black fur starkly contrasted the snow, which enabled her to see him. The wind blew so hard that she could hardly hear her own voice when she called out to her friend up ahead. In fact, she thought that she should have brought a walking stick of her own. Fall had to hunch over to press forward. She nearly had to crawl at times, to fight against the strength of the wind.

When Fall realized it was no use to call out to Drizzle any longer, she focused entirely on trying to keep up her pace. She could not allow her friend out of her sight. In this kind of a storm, she was greatly concerned that Drizzle would get lost and be stranded all alone in the middle of the squall without knowing how to get back home. However, Fall was not sure how to get back herself. The wind quickly erased any and all signs of their presence. Her footprints were completely undetectable in the swirling snow.

Fall gasped when Drizzle was no longer in sight. Her fears had become reality. *Oh no!* Fall thought to herself. In a panic, she shouted for him repeatedly. "Drizzle! Drizzle! Where are you? It's me! Fall!" She paused for a moment then tried again. "Drizzle! Answer me!" She realized that her shouts were of no use.

Fall raced across the snow, toward Drizzle's last known location, but she still could not catch a glimpse of her friend. A tear trickled down her cheek and quickly became ice. "Drizzle!" she wept softly. As Fall continued further, she felt hopeless. She cried harder. Fall worried for Drizzle, and for herself as well.

Fall traversed the land the best she could, though the terrain now sloped away. Without warning, Fall slipped and tumbled down the hill. She slid to a stop, stood up, and brushed the snow off. The wind blew so hard that it was impossible for her to see the terrain or to know where the clouds stopped and the ground began. Fear gripped tightly upon the young cub's heart. She screamed, "Help me! Help! Please help!" Fall attempted to turn back, but continued to slide back down the hill.

Fall lay in the snow. Her hope fled from her. She had no idea what she'd do next. She lifted her head, wiped snow from her eyes, and saw a shadowy figure come toward her. She stood up and put her paws over her eyes to shield them from the snow. She hoped it would allow her to get a better look. Before long, the figure stood right in front of her.

"Fall? What are you doing here?" Drizzle asked.

"I came to get you!" Fall struggled to reply through the turmoil of the storm.

"Why? I'm on a dangerous mission! You shouldn't have come!" Drizzle insisted.

"Drizzle, I'm worried about you! Come back with me," Fall beckoned.

"I can't! I have to prove that I'm not worthless. I want my parents and Flurry to see that I can be brave and courageous, too."

"Drizzle, you don't have to prove anything to anybody! I'm your friend, and you didn't need to prove anything to me."

"You wouldn't understand."

"Okay, now you sound like my brother," Fall shot back. "You're more like him than you …" Before their conversation could continue, they heard a bloodcurdling howl. "Uh … what was that?" Fall asked in an uneasy tone.

"It sounded like a wolf," Drizzle replied with concern in his voice.

"Drizzle, I'm scared!" Fall ran up and grabbed his arm.

"Come with me! I think I found a place where we can take shelter." Drizzle led Fall by the paw. They pressed forward and disappeared into the blanket of heavy snowfall.

Meanwhile, Vallidore continued to howl. "I hope they can hear me and call back to us," Vallidore told the cubs who rode on his back. They continued on their course toward Ursidea.

"Unless they hear your howl, and it scares them away," Flurry reasoned.

"You have a point. I'll redouble my effort to get us there sooner," answered the white wolf. Vallidore added another burst of speed to his hot pursuit of their friends.

Vallidore ran as fast, if not faster, than any wolf could run, but the deep snow made it difficult for him. His muscles ached as the icy precipitation continued to descend from the sky with no end in sight. Vallidore was without any footprints to track. Luckily, he knew the land very well, and he could find Ursidea with his eyes closed.

"We're almost there! Both of you keep your eyes sharp. This land is very dangerous. There's a good reason why

Christopher made this region forbidden."

"Why?" Flurry asked. "What's so bad about it?"

"Have you heard of Jack Frost?" Vallidore asked.

"Uhm … I'm not sure. Kind of. I guess?"

"Ages ago, Jack and Christopher were friends, but Jack became evil. At the peak of his tyranny, Jack ruled all of the northern lands from his throne in Ursidea. Jack was cruel and unrelenting. He demanded homage from everyone. Those not loyal to him were hunted down and brought to justice. Well, it was what he considered to be justice anyway.

"It seemed like his cruel and twisted rule would never end, until one brave warrior challenged him. A red panda, by the name of Tomodachi the Great, dared to dispute

Jack's reigning dictatorship. Christopher Kringle sought the help of the Great King. The King gave a special sword to Christopher and asked that it be delivered to Tomodachi. This sword was forged by the blue stars of Khima. It's said that the sword has the power to defeat evil regardless of what form it may take. Tomodachi and Jack had a final confrontation in Ursidea. Tomodachi and a bear cub defeated Jack together. Jack was imprisoned in his palace and buried. He has remained there for the past 7,000 years."

"If he's in prison, then we don't have anything to worry about," Flurry concluded. "We don't, right?"

"Christopher is worried that Jack might be free. The weather was his first point of concern. It has never gotten this cold, nor has there been a blizzard since the time of Jack's rule. He's either free, or it's a sign that his evil is awakening."

"Uh, oh!" Flurry's face expressed an immense amount of fear. Noah listened intently to every detail of the story. When he noticed that Flurry looked worried, he patted him on the arm to reassure the cub that he was there to watch over him.

Suddenly, they came to a stop. "There!" Vallidore called out.

"What?" Flurry asked.

"We're near Jack's palace. However, this is a bad sign. I don't see Drizzle or Fall. They're either lost, or they've gone inside. Both outcomes are bad. Hold on tight! We need to go down and make sure they haven't gone into the palace."

Vallidore rushed down the hill. This was

the very same slope that Fall slid down only moments prior, but all signs of her presence were erased by the snow and wind.

When they ascended another hill, Flurry saw something out ahead of them that glimmered. "Look!" Flurry shouted and jumped off of Vallidore's back to run toward the shimmering object.

Noah was horrified by Flurry's haste. He, too, alighted from Vallidore's back. The lion cub waved his arms back and forth to warn Flurry of danger, but the bear cub did not listen, as usual. Flurry scurried out onto what seemed to be fresh ice.

"Why isn't this covered by snow?" Flurry asked the wolf. Before Vallidore could reply, the ice cracked, and Flurry fell through.

"Flurry!" Vallidore shouted, sped up to

the edge of the broken ice, and peered down into the hole. It was too dark for the wolf to see anything clearly.

"I'm okay!" came Flurry's soft, faint voice.

Noah felt relieved, but Vallidore's concern grew more dire. "Flurry! Stay where you are! Noah and I will find another way down. Stay put! I mean it!"

Vallidore and Noah rushed down the hill to search for another entry point. The terrain had changed a lot over the years, but Vallidore realized that the giant mound of snow was, in fact, Jack's buried palace. Vallidore was deeply troubled by how imminent the danger really was. Jack lived long before Vallidore was born, but the wolf knew full well the horrible things Frost had done. Jack would not hesitate to kill anyone, not even a cub. Vallidore hoped that Flurry would do as he was told, for once, and stay put.

However, Flurry was far too inquisitive to simply stand by and do nothing. When his eyes adjusted to the cave's dark surroundings, he was able to make out the silhouettes of statues, columns, and arches. The hole up above helped. It allowed rays of light to beam down into the cave. Flurry stumbled through the dimly lit room before he came upon a torch mounted on the wall. Flurry still had his flint stones that Wolfhroc had given him from his last adventure. The only problem was that Flurry was not tall enough to reach it.

He pondered how to obtain the torch when something startled him. Flurry froze in place. He was not alone. The sound of footsteps approached. A chill shot down Flurry's body, and his fur stood on end. "Doggy? Is that you? Doggy?" The cub jerked his head to and fro with each sound that echoed across the stone walls. His heart sank as fear gripped him further.

Flurry thought he saw movement, but was unsure. He peered out into the distant darkness, but could not make anything out. *Maybe it was just a statue*, Flurry thought to himself. Flurry was content with that explanation until he saw it move. There was no mistake. Flurry was convinced that he was not alone in the darkness. The dark, shadowy figure moved closer. Flurry backed up. His movement alerted the other, and it came toward him quickly. "Ahhh!" Flurry screamed.

Flurry's bellow caused a rumble in the

cave, and icicles crashed down from the ceiling. The commotion knocked Flurry and the dark figure to the ground. *This is my chance!* Flurry thought to himself. The cub decided to gain the upper paw on the mysterious visitor while they lay on the ground – momentarily stunned from the fall. Flurry launched himself at the figure and tackled it. "Gotcha!" Flurry shouted in victory.

"Ouch! Flurry! Get off! It's me! Drizzle!"

A bit surprised, Flurry ceased his grip. "Oh! Sorry, Drizzle. I didn't know it was you. What are you doing here?" Flurry asked.

Drizzle stood up, brushed the dust off of his fur, and answered. "I could ask you the same thing. Right now, I'm looking for a light source. Your sister is trapped in some sort of room, and I can't read the symbols on the door to figure out how to free her."

"Symbols? What symbols? What does that have to do with freeing my sister?"

"I think this place is booby-trapped. I could free Fall if I could just read the markings, but it's too dark in here."

"This should be a good thing. I thought you hate light?" Flurry sarcastically remarked.

"Really? You want to do this now? I'm trying to save your sister, and you make fun of me!" Drizzle shook his head and walked away.

Flurry sighed and followed after him. "Well, I have flint, so we could light a torch. Wolfhroc taught me how to do it."

"Who?"

"Never mind! Just help me reach that

torch!" Flurry pointed up at his target.

"How?" Drizzle asked.

"Let me stand on your shoulders. I think I can reach it."

"No, you can't."

"Yes, I can."

"No! You can't!"

"Why do you always have to argue with me?" Flurry shouted.

"I'm not trying to argue with you. I'm only stating a fact," Drizzle defended.

"Oh, so now you think you know it all?"

"I never said that I know it all. I'm just saying that you cannot reach that torch even if you were standing on my shoulders," Drizzle tried to articulate his meaning.

"Well, somebody is Mister Glass Half Empty!"

"No! You don't understand! You and I

are each eighteen inches tall. If you stood on top of my head, that would give us a combined height of three feet. The torch on the wall is at least five feet from the ground. There's no way we can reach it. We need to find another light source or something to stand on to give us some additional height."

Flurry did not know what to say. He always considered conversations with Drizzle to be so laborious. The black-furred bear frequently misunderstood dialogue, and conveyed or interpreted everything literally.

Flurry went along with Drizzle's plan, and they explored the cave for anything that would aid them. They were about to give up when they entered a large open room with a pedestal at the center. The room had a domed roof and an arcade that encircled the space.

"Look!" Flurry shouted. The cub's outburst caused the stone to rumble. Ice cracked and echoed throughout the adjoined chambers.

"Uh … Flurry? Maybe you shouldn't shout so loud," Drizzle advised with a cautious tone.

"Yeah, I'll have to agree with you on that one," Flurry replied. "Look at that! There's something glowing over there!"

Flurry and Drizzle rushed over to the pedestal together. There they found a golden-yellow gemstone which glowed and shimmered while it hovered in the air. "How do you suppose it floats like that?" Drizzle asked.

"I don't know! Who cares? It's very pretty though." Flurry was completely mesmerized by the jewel. "Ooooh!" was the only thing Flurry said. He was so entranced that he did not even blink.

Drizzle leaned forward and waved his paw in front of Flurry's face. "Flurry, come on! We need to go help your sister. Grab it and let's go."

"Right!" Flurry stretched his paw toward the gemstone, but it was slightly out of his reach. "That rock over there! It should be enough to boost me up." Flurry shuffled over to the nearby stone and pushed it toward the pedestal.

Drizzle would have helped Flurry, but something caught his attention. There was a plaque on the pedestal covered in ice. "Flurry! Look at this!"

Flurry stopped what he was doing and rushed over to look where Drizzle had pointed. Flurry picked up a small stone and smashed it against the ice. The frozen sheet broke away and fell to the ground. Drizzle brushed the remaining fragments away from the plaque. "What does it say?" Flurry asked.

"What do you mean? Can't you read?" Drizzle responded.

"Of course I can! I was just testing you to see if you could or not," Flurry dishonestly replied. He still had not learned, but was too prideful to admit it in front of Drizzle.

Drizzle, on the other hand, was adept with his reading skills for a cub his age. "It looks like a riddle. It says, 'Frozen in time, Frost will keep. Deep underground, Jack will sleep. By the origin paw, may the ice be moved. If so you do, all will be doomed. Beautiful and lovely, the gem may be. Remove it and find trouble indeed.' I wonder what that means."

In haste, Flurry answered, "Not important. Now help me with this rock!"

"Flurry, I think we need to be careful in here. This place isn't safe."

"Whatever. Be a wimp. I don't care."

Flurry's comment cut to the heart. Grieved, a tear fell from Drizzle's eye and landed on the plaque below. Drizzle wiped the tear off to find a second set of engraved letters. "Flurry! There's more!"

Drizzle brushed the second set of text off and found a single sentence which startled him. He scratched his head and glanced back and forth between the text and Flurry. It did not seem possible. Drizzle read it again: "Flurry, don't even think about it!" The cub's eyes widened, and his mouth fell ajar. Why did this engraved text have Flurry's name on it? How could such an old place know about Flurry? "Flurry! You have to see this!"

"Not now, Drizzle! I almost have the rock in place, no thanks to you, I might add." Flurry panted and gasped for breath while he pushed the stone. Doing it by himself was difficult and taxing for the little fellow.

"Flurry! This is important! It mentions you!"

"What? That's not possible! Where?" Flurry rushed up to look.

"It says, 'Flurry, don't even think about it!'"

"Yeah, right! You're just making that up. Really funny, Drizzle! Really funny!" Flurry was irritated that Drizzle would make such a poor attempt at a joke. Flurry shook it off and pushed the stone up to the pedestal.

"Would you two stop arguing and help me?" shouted a female voice in the distance. Suddenly the cave rumbled, and ice shattered and fell down around them.

Flurry realized that their voices carried pretty far inside the cave, and that his sister could hear him from whatever room she was currently trapped in. Flurry blushed and answered his sister. "So you heard all of that, huh?"

"Yes! Now hurry up and get me out of here!" Fall bellowed. Her action made more ice crumble and smash down from above. The place shook hard enough that Flurry and Drizzle both stumbled to the ground.

Before Drizzle had a chance to recover, Flurry had already returned to his task. He reached for the glowing, yellow crystal. "Flurry, no!" shouted a distant voice, but it was too late. Flurry grabbed the radiant stone. He looked up from his paw, which now held the gem. It had changed from emitting yellow light to blue. Flurry saw Vallidore and Noah off in the distance.

The entire cave shook, and an evil laugh echoed throughout the cavern walls. Icicles fell all around them. The floor cracked and gave way. Stones shoved out from the walls, which caused them to buckle. The entire place was falling apart. Flurry and Drizzle could barely stand while the ground shook vigorously.

"Help me!" Fall shouted. Flurry and Drizzle rushed to the wall that Fall was trapped behind.

"Stop! You must be careful about this! If she's caught in one of Jack's traps, the wrong button or switch could end her life!"

Vallidore shouted.

"Now that we have some light, I believe I can do this," Drizzle answered.

"We need to free her and get out of here quickly! The whole place is coming down around us!" the wolf replied.

Vallidore was correct. The stone roof was collapsing, and rocks dropped more frequently. "Hurry!" Fall screamed.

"We're here! We're here! We're going to get you out! Just hold on!" Drizzle called out to her. "Flurry, hold up the light so I can see."

Flurry did as Drizzle instructed. The crystal's light revealed a peculiar locking mechanism on the door. There was a square indentation in place of a typical lock. Within the recess of the strange lock were many differently-sized rectangular shapes that were able to slide in different directions. "What kind of a lock is this?" Flurry asked. "What ever happened to using a key?"

"It's a puzzle lock. This is very common in the land of Nallan Min. That's where Jack is from," Vallidore answered. "It can only be opened by sliding the pieces in the right direction. If you do it the wrong way, it will undoubtedly activate a deathtrap that would certainly spell doom for Fall."

"I'm good at games! Let me try!" Flurry ran up and started to fiddle with the puzzle lock faster than anyone could react.

"No!" shouted Drizzle and Vallidore in unison, but it was too late. Flurry had activated the trap – this much was obvious when Fall screamed.

"Flurry, help me! The ceiling is coming down on me!" Fall cried as the room got smaller and smaller.

Drizzle pushed Flurry out of the way, "Let me do this!"

"Hey!" Flurry replied.

Noah quickly grabbed Flurry and pulled him back. "Noah is correct! Let Drizzle do it!" Vallidore ordered.

Time ticked away. The walls of the cave collapsed further. Stones collided with the floor and sprayed fragments of rock in every direction. Drizzle's paws moved speedily. He continued to maneuver the different pieces of the puzzle lock.

The top of the room drew nearer to Fall's head. "Guys! I'm going to be crushed! Please hurry!"

There was no reply. Fall could not hear anything except the rumbling of the walls as they gave way. Fall sat in a corner with her arms wrapped around her legs. Her hope of survival dwindled. She buried her face between her knees and cried.

The stone roof continued to draw nearer with each second. It now touched the top of her head. Fall lay down flat on the floor, and attempted to call out to her brother once more. Tears streamed down her cream-colored fur.

"Flurry, tell Mama and Papa I love them, and that I'm so sorry!" She paused momentarily to sob. "Oh, and Flurry, despite our differences I love you very much!" Fall did not hear a reply. "Flurry? Flurry?" She screamed, "Flurry!" Her death was imminent. The room continued to shrink. In a brief moment Fall would be crushed.

She closed her eyes and bawled. Fall braced herself for the inevitable. The rock surface inched down and pressed against her ears, but suddenly ceased. The ceiling reversed its direction, and quickly returned to its original spot.

The door opened. "Come on!" shouted Flurry and Drizzle together. They beckoned for her to come out of the room. Tears of joy came down from her eyes. She smiled and bolted out of the room as quickly as she could.

"We have to go! Now!" Vallidore shouted.

"So soon?" echoed an evil voice.

"Uh, what was that?" Flurry asked uneasily.

They all froze in their tracks. Vallidore turned to look in the direction of the pedestal. Just beyond it stood two stone statues, and between the statues were steps that led up to a throne. The throne was not clearly visible, since it had been covered in ice. As Vallidore stared at the ice-covered throne, cracks formed across it. The wolf looked back at the cubs and shouted, "Run!"

They ran as fast as they could, but the ground shook so much that they kept falling. Stone and ice continued to shatter everywhere. It was clear that the entire palace would cave in very soon. Each step they took was riddled with danger. In fact, Flurry would have been crushed if it had not been for Noah. The lion leapt and shoved Flurry out of the path of a falling stone.

It looked like they would make it. They were near the opening of the cave, when tragedy struck. The roof fell down behind the cubs and sealed Vallidore inside.

"Doggy!" Flurry shouted.

"Oh no! What are we going to do?" Fall asked.

"Vallidore knew the risks. He ordered us to escape. We need to respect his wishes," Drizzle answered.

"We can't leave Doggy behind!" Flurry insisted.

"The reason he came here was to ensure our safety. Going back puts us at risk again," Drizzle tried to reason.

"You're just saying that because you're a coward!" Flurry shot his insult at Drizzle.

"No, I'm not!"

"Yes, you are!"

Fall interjected before the argument got worse. "Both of you, stop it! I'm so sick of you two fighting all of the time! This wouldn't even be happening if you two weren't always bickering with each other! I think what we should do is head back to Mr. Kringle's house and get help."

"That would take too long! It took us hours to get here. It will be late in the evening by the time we make it to Ursus, and then it would be early tomorrow morning before we could return to save Vallidore," Drizzle explained.

Flurry ran to the caved-in entrance, and pulled loose stones away to make an opening for himself. Tears flowed freely from his eyes. Flurry sobbed. "I don't care what anyone says! I'm going in to save him! Hang on, Doggy! Hang on! I'm coming!"

CHAPTER 4
AN ANCIENT EVIL

Evening hours fast approached. The sky was still blanketed by the storm clouds, though the heavy snow had abated. Christopher peered out the window of his study and examined the terrain for any sign of the little cubs. Catherine rapped on the door and entered. "I have horses prepared, should we need them. Would you like me to fetch your sword?" asked the tall redhead. She stood at the study's open entryway.

Christopher turned his troubled face

toward her. "I fear that no preparation will be enough, dear Catherine. The last time we stood against Jack, it tore all of the regions apart with war. I guess peace just wasn't meant to last forever."

"Sweetheart, you've done your best, and you've kept the peace for thousands of years. No one is perfect, and you can't predict every possible outcome. We should make the best of whatever this new stage of life brings us. After all, if your hunch is correct, you made the right choice in allowing Flurry to lead this quest to stop Jack." Catherine's words succeeded. Christopher stood up straight, took in a deep breath, and smiled.

He glanced back at Catherine. When he caught the glimmer in her eyes, he felt strong again. "You're right! I shall retrieve my sword at once." He walked over to his lady, embraced her, and gave her a kiss. "I'll do everything in my power to protect you and all that are within my domain. Thank you for reminding me that there's always hope, even when things look this bleak."

"I love you!"

Christopher walked past his wife and out through the door before he briefly stopped to reply to her parting words. "I love you, too! Now, and always!"

In the banquet hall, the bears were still gathered together. They were alarmed about the events from earlier in the day. Caboose had decided to go on a mission to find Flurry. He knew Flurry must be in the house somewhere. *Flurry must be playing hide-and-seek again*, Caboose thought to himself. "Flurry! Oh Flurry! Where are you hiding?

I'm going to find you."

"He isn't hiding, Caboose!" Boaz insisted. "He left with Noah and Vallidore on a mission."

"On a mission to hide, I bet!" Caboose replied.

"No! On a mission to … oh, never mind!" After numerous attempts, Boaz had given up on trying to get Caboose to understand that Flurry was not in the house.

Caboose wandered down a long hallway in his search for Flurry. Boaz was concerned that Caboose would get himself into trouble, so he decided to follow along. "Come on, Honja, we can't let him roam the halls alone," Boaz said and motioned for the little brown rabbit to follow him. Honja shook his head, but Boaz would not take no for an answer. Honja was about to take a bite out of his carrot he had acquired from the vast array of food still out on the tables. Before Honja bit down, Boaz snatched it away from the rabbit's paws and dangled it in front of his face.

"*Nae tanggŭn eya!*" Honja called out in his native tongue. Boaz had learned to speak Honja's language so that he could communicate with him, but nobody else could understand what Honja ever said.

"No, I'm not giving you the carrot until you come with us." Boaz scurried down the hall after Caboose, and brought Honja's carrot along with him. Honja sat there angrily for a bit before he realized that he had been left all alone in the room. The cold wind could be heard against the windows, and a chill came over him. Honja felt uneasy to be left all alone. The rabbit sighed, quickly hopped along after Boaz and Caboose, and shouted, "*Gah-chi gah!*"

Back at the cave in Ursidea, things looked grim. Vallidore awoke from his brief moment of unconscious. One of the stones had struck him in the head. Though his vision was a bit blurry, Vallidore stood up. He pawed at the pile of rubble that covered the exit. Faint voices could be heard from outside. The wolf made out one of the voices to be Flurry. He looked around and noticed that the cave now had much more light than before. Bits of the roof had collapsed entirely which let light shine in. Thankfully, the sun remained up, despite the late hour of the evening. Ursidea was not far enough south for the sun to have completely set. Vallidore was grateful for that fact. To look for an exit in the darkness of night would have been far more dangerous. *Maybe I can find a different way out*, the wolf thought to himself.

Without wasting a single moment, the white wolf rushed to find an alternate outlet. The cave was very unstable, but the rocks had ceased their descent for the time being. The cavern still shook and rumbled from time-to-time.

Vallidore knew he had to get out soon, before the rest of the stone and ice eventually collapsed. He saw an opening in the wall. The wolf darted across the room. However, Vallidore's pursuit of his exit came to a sudden halt. The wolf spun back around and rushed up to where the pedestal stood. He had to be sure that his eyes were not playing tricks on him. Unfortunately, they were not. Just beyond where the wolf stood sat an empty throne. The ice had broken away, and the one who sat upon said throne was nowhere to be found.

"What? You don't see what you were expecting to find?" a voice called out from the shadows. The wolf spun around and found Jack Frost standing before him. Jack was a red panda, and compared to Vallidore, he was very small. However, he was not one you would want to judge by his size, for what he lacked in height, he more than made up for in evil and cunning.

Regardless of his stature, he wielded the power to control the cold and ice. He could use them as a weapon, and Jack did exactly that. Before Vallidore could react, Jack outstretched his arms and caused the white wolf to be struck down by a chillingly strong gust of wind mixed with ice fragments.

Some of the ice cut into the wolf, as if broken shards of glass were being hurled at him.

"It'll take more than that to keep me down!" Vallidore growled and leapt at the red panda. Jack was unimpressed. With a motion of his paw, icicles broke free from the wall and flew toward the wolf.

Many chunks of ice hit Vallidore before he managed to bat some of them out of his way with his big, burly paws. He focused his attention back on Jack, but the red panda was too fast. Vallidore attempted to pounce on or strike his red-furred opponent, but Jack managed to jump over, slide under, or dodge every attack the wolf threw at him.

In a condescending tone, Jack commented, "Seriously? You'll have to do better than that! I'm the greatest threat

Christopher Kringle has ever faced, and he sends you? If this is the best he's got, his downfall is closer than he thinks." Jack behaved as though he was in a place of authority and the wolf was there for a school lesson.

Vallidore continued to attack, but this time, Jack pulled a sword from the scabbard at his side and swung it at his rival.

"So you think you need a sword to defeat me?" Vallidore taunted.

"No. I need to make a point, if you know what I mean." With a quick sweep of his arm, Jack sliced Vallidore across the side of his snout.

Vallidore leapt back, licked his wound, and growled at Jack. If it were anyone other than Frost, Vallidore would have greatly intimidated them with his sharp, razor-like teeth bared at his enemy. With his piercing blue eyes, he stared the red panda down. However, Jack was a battle-hardened warrior, and one wolf was not a concern to him at all. He raised his blade for another advance. Jack swung again, just as Vallidore leapt at him. A slight whimper was heard when Jack cut Vallidore on the side of his leg.

Jack addressed his adversary. "I must say, you're sure taking your sweet time about dying, aren't you? Let's speed things up a bit, shall we? I have an appointment I intend to keep."

"The only appointment you'll be keeping is with the grave!" Vallidore's wit kicked in.

"We shall see!" Jack drew back into a defensive stance. He was prepared to strike at any moment.

Vallidore was a great and valiant warrior, but Jack was something that very few could truly handle. Misjudge him by his size, and that would be the last mistake you ever made. There was a special line of warriors known as The Protectors who were trained to handle a threat like Jack. Vallidore knew that he needed to find at least one of The Protectors if he were to truly stop a villain like Frost.

Vallidore growled and crouched into an attack posture of his own. The wolf hoped that Jack would assume he was going to pounce. The plan was that he would leap for the exit as soon as Jack made his move.

However, Jack was smarter than Vallidore gave him credit. The wicked red panda was a master strategist, and he knew Vallidore would attempt an escape. Jack played along, and ran toward Vallidore. The wolf leapt toward the exit, but got the wind knocked out of him when a surprise attack came from seemingly nowhere. Jack kicked Vallidore square in the chest, struck him again on the snout, and then cut the wolf yet again. The final bladed strike opened a wound on the side of Vallidore's face.

The three swift attacks knocked Vallidore to the ground. The wolf lay on the cold stone, dazed and out of breath. He looked up and saw Jack approach. The red panda stood on some collapsed stones. Now elevated above the wolf, Jack turned the point of his sword downward. He prepared to finish Vallidore, once and for all.

Vallidore could not believe it would end this way. Thousands of years of peace were about to end with his own death. He struggled to get up, but Jack shoved him back down with his foot. The wolf's fur was stained blue with his own blood. "Say goodbye," Jack commanded the wounded wolf.

"Okay, goodbye!" came a small voice from across the throne room just as a stone struck Jack in the head. The impact caused the red panda to drop his sword and collapse to the ground. "Now Doggy! Now! Run!" Flurry yelled.

Vallidore jumped to his feet and ran toward Flurry. Jack stood back up and shook his head in his attempt to regain his senses. Flurry had struck Jack hard enough with the rock that he struggled to get back to his feet. From the red panda's perspective, the stone seemed to come out of nowhere.

Jack's vision refocused. He turned and

saw Flurry and Vallidore attempt to escape. At the sight of Flurry, Jack's face instantly changed from confusion to extreme anger and frustration. "You! You! You! What does it take to destroy you? Ahhh!" Jack was suddenly furious and lost all control of his senses at the sight of Flurry. The bear cub had somehow hit a nerve with Jack. A deep emotional response was triggered in the usually calm and collected villain.

The room shook and the walls crumbled all around. Jack's scream and the increased weight of the snow from the storm caused the collapse of the buried palace to resume. Vallidore and Flurry ran for the newly opened exit that Flurry and Drizzle had dug together. Jack picked up his sword and chased after them. By his command, icicles rose up all around them. Jack attempted to cut them off from their exit with the ice, but Flurry and Vallidore had a head start on him. They made it to the exit and crawled out just as the cave collapsed in on Jack.

Rumbling and thundering could be heard as dust and debris coughed out of the cracks between the fallen rocks. "Yay! We did it!" Flurry exclaimed.

"Don't be so hasty," Vallidore spoke softly, for he was now very weak.

"Are you okay, Mr. Doggy?" Flurry asked.

"I'll be fine," the wolf lied. "They're superficial wounds. What's important is that we find The Protectors as soon as possible. Only they can defeat Jack."

"I wouldn't be so sure. We may no longer need them. I don't know anyone that can survive a cave-in like that," Fall chimed in.

"Don't underestimate him. I did, and that's how I was just defeated. I think precautions need to be taken, just in case he survived."

"We could always go back in and look," Drizzle suggested.

Noah did not like that idea, and waved his arms back and forth while he shook his head "no".

"Yeah, I'm with Noah on that one," Flurry remarked.

"All of you need to head back to Christopher and warn him. I'll go in search of The Protectors. This way, we have a better chance of success. Jack's first priority will be to attack Kringle's territory," Vallidore insisted.

"Uh … I don't mean to disagree, but you're in no shape to go alone." Fall voiced her concern.

"I think I should go with you," Drizzle volunteered.

"Well, if he's going with you, then so am I!" Flurry shouted, for he was not about to be outdone by Drizzle.

Noah buried his face in his paws out of sheer disbelief.

"We can't all go with Vallidore. Who will warn the others?" Fall reasoned.

"You can!" Flurry replied.

"How typical of you, Flurry! Of course you don't want your sister to go along! This whole mess is your fault anyway!" Fall screamed back at her brother.

"All the more reason for me to go with Doggy, so I can fix it!"

Vallidore realized the conversation was going nowhere fast, and someone needed to be the voice of reason and authority. "Fall, will you be able to go back and warn the others?"

Fall hesitated. "Yes, I should be fine ... I think. Why?" she asked.

"Time is against us. We cannot afford to stay here and debate this. These three shall come with me, for I may need their help if we have another confrontation with Jack. You're quick on your feet, and we need to send warning back to Christopher so that your family and friends won't be taken by surprise if Jack attacks. Believe me, if he survived, he will attack."

"Okay, but how will I find my way? Our tracks are gone."

Vallidore paused for a moment to think. While in thought he noticed the staff that Drizzle held. "Where did you get that?"

Vallidore shouted at the cub.

"Ouch! Not so loud! That hurts my ears," Drizzle replied.

"I'm sorry, but I need to know. Where did you get that staff? It looks like one of Christopher's staffs."

"It is. I grabbed it when I snuck out. I intended to return it to him. I was only borrowing it," Drizzle assured the wolf.

"You aren't in trouble. In fact, we're very fortunate that you grabbed this particular one. It would seem that the Great King is with us this day after all. This staff is named Path Finder. It leads its bearer to their intended destination without fail. Anyone using the staff will never get lost. Would you please lend it to Fall? It will guide her back safely."

"Sure!" Drizzle handed Fall the staff. The

cubs exchanged hugs and waved goodbye to Fall as she began her journey back to Ursus. Flurry, Drizzle, and Noah climbed onto Vallidore's back. The wolf raced off across the snow toward the south and called out to The Protectors with his howls.

Fall pushed on toward her home alone, with only Christopher Kringle's staff to guide her. The trip seemed to take forever – as it always seemed when one found themselves in an emergency. Hours later, she managed to reach the Kringles' house, and stumbled up to knock on the door. It was answered by a bear who held a mug of hot tea in his paw. He wore glasses and had a yellow crescent moon shape on his chest which sharply contrasted his red fur.

"Hello, Jinja," Fall addressed the crimson-colored bear.

"Let her in already!" came another voice. A purple and white panda bear named Mojo spoke up. Mojo and Jinja were great friends, but they constantly bickered with each other.

"I was going to let her in!" Jinja shot back at Mojo.

"Oh. So that's why she's still standing outside?" Mojo answered sarcastically.

"I'm letting her in now!"

"It doesn't look like it to me."

"Be quiet!"

"You be quiet!"

"Uh … guys … I really need to see Mr. Kringle. It's important," Fall interrupted.

"Right! Of course! Come in," Jinja replied and shut the door behind her. He led the cub to Christopher's study and knocked at the door.

"Enter!" came the voice from inside.

Fall stepped through the door and addressed the man who stood with his back to her while he gazed out the window. "Mr. Kringle?"

Christopher turned and saw Fall. He immediately rushed over to her and knelt down to give her his full attention. "My dear! Where have you been? Where are Drizzle and Flurry? Are they okay? Please tell me you have good news."

"Uh … well, actually, I don't. Sorry." Fall shifted her gaze down to the floor. Her chin quivered.

"Don't cry, my dear, it'll be okay. Tell me everything," Christopher's voice consoled her.

"Well, you see, Drizzle wanted to prove that he's valuable by doing something brave. He found this cave, and we went inside. I don't know what else happened, because I got trapped in a scary room. Someone named Jack escaped somehow, and attacked Vallidore. Vallidore got hurt really badly, but he insisted that he was fine. I knew he was lying to me. He told me to come back and warn everyone that Jack got free and is planning to attack you. Vallidore went to find The Protectors or something like that. Flurry and Drizzle insisted on going with him, so they are all with Vallidore right now."

Fear was prominently displayed upon Christopher's face as he listened to Fall. However, he quickly regained his wits. The man firmed his upper lip, stood back up, and ordered Jinja to fetch his wife. When Catherine came in, Christopher was quick with his instructions. "We have trouble! Go and send word to the elves that Jack Frost is free and likely to attack us. Send out your scouts and anything else that must be done. I'll join you shortly." Catherine nodded and rushed out of the room.

Fall stood there and cried. "I'm so sorry! We didn't mean to do this."

"There, there, now, it's not your fault." Christopher reached down, picked up the little cub, and set her on his lap as he took a seat in his chair. "Nobody is to blame here. It was only a matter of time before this happened. Together we're strong, and together we can defeat him. We've done so before, and we can do it again. Now, let's go reunite you with your parents."

Christopher set her back down and led her to the banquet hall where her parents had gathered with the other bears. "Fall!" her parents shouted. They ran up and hugged their daughter. "How's Flurry? Is he okay? Where is he?" they both asked.

"Yes, he's fine. Well, he is for now anyway," Fall mentioned as her eyes filled with tears again.

Fall's parents looked down at their daughter and squeezed her tightly. "Well, at least you're safe with us now. Let's hope that Flurry will return to us safely, too."

CHAPTER 5
CHINGU THE PROTECTOR

Vallidore was still on the run. The trio had worked their way south throughout the night. It was clear to the cubs that they were far from home due to the change in the sun's behavior. The bright ball of flame worked its way from the horizon to cast a radiant yellow hue upon the landscape. At this point, Vallidore had run for far too long. He needed to rest, but he could not bring himself to stop. Too much was at risk. He pressed further. The wolf deceived himself into believing that he would take a break soon, in order to persevere a little longer. *After the next clearing*, he thought to himself, but rest never came.

Vallidore and the cubs had long been out of the frozen land of Ursidea. Hours had passed since they entered a lush and beautiful forest. The ground was littered with purple flowers.

Flurry felt hungry and could not believe he had gone the night without food. "Doggy! I'm hungry!" Flurry bellowed.

"Me, too!" added Drizzle.

Vallidore did not reply. He had only stopped briefly to drink. Beyond that, the wolf had continued through the thick bushes and in between branches with the single goal of reaching one of The Protectors.

Despite Vallidore's speed, strength, and

willpower, he could not keep this up for long. He had lost a lot of blood, and his wounds were untended. His eyelids became heavy, and before anyone knew what had happened, the valiant wolf collapsed. Vallidore's fall tossed the cubs from his back and into a thicket.

"Ouch!" Flurry complained when he sat up and rubbed his head. He looked around and found Drizzle face down in a mud puddle, kicking his legs.

Flurry got up and ran over to Drizzle. Together, Flurry and Noah pulled Drizzle out of the mud. "Of course this would happen to me," Drizzle grumbled.

"Hee, hee, hee, hee, hee!" Flurry giggled.

"It's not funny!"

"Yes, it is!"

Drizzle crossed his arms and pouted.

Noah rushed over to check on Vallidore. The lion stood up and motioned for the bear cubs to come quickly. Flurry and Drizzle jumped up and made haste to Vallidore's side.

"Is he okay?" Flurry asked.

"He's breathing, but it's very shallow," Drizzle observed.

"He needs help!" Flurry insisted. The cub's chin quivered. He fought back his tears as best he could.

"Well, obviously! But what are we supposed to do? I'm not a doctor, are you?" Drizzle replied.

"You don't have to be rude about it!" Flurry snapped back.

Drizzle was about to escalate the argument, but Noah ran up and extended his arms to separate the cubs. Then he pointed at his eyes and then out at the tree line.

"What is it, Noah? Do you see something?" Flurry inquired.

Noah nodded his head. Flurry and Drizzle became tense. They quickly took cover behind a rock and looked around cautiously. *Could Jack have caught up with us so fast?* Flurry wondered.

"What do you see?" Drizzle whispered.

"Nothing," Flurry replied. "Do you see anything?"

"Nope."

Just then there was the sound of a snapped twig. Flurry turned his head toward the sound and caught a glimpse of a furry animal on the branch of a nearby tree. "There!" Flurry pointed in the direction of their visitor.

"Oh! I see it, too!" Drizzle affirmed.

"Noah, do you see it?" Flurry turned around and found Noah absent from their hiding spot. "Uh, oh. I hope Jack didn't get him!" Flurry looked around frantically to figure out Noah's whereabouts, but his fear was relieved when he realized Noah had circled out and around the trees to try to flank the intruder. "Good thinking, Noah," Flurry murmured to himself. Unfortunately, Noah's shrewd plan caused Flurry to concoct the terrible idea of being a decoy.

Flurry stood up and walked out into the clearing next to Vallidore and hummed loudly.

"What are you doing?" Drizzle whispered.

"Just humming. Why?"

"Get back here where it's safe!" Drizzle insisted.

"Why?"

"It's dangerous!"

"What? Danger is my middle n ..." Flurry was about say "name", but the figure suddenly jumped down from the tree. Flurry screamed, and leapt back behind the rock with Drizzle.

"Smooth, Flurry! Really smooth!" Drizzle poked at his companion. Flurry looked at him and grinned nervously.

The cubs watched on with fear. It was a red panda, no doubt about it. He also had a weapon. The cubs feared that Jack had come to finish them off.

As the stranger drew closer, it became apparent to Flurry that this was not Jack. Flurry and Drizzle looked up and saw a different red panda tending to Vallidore's wounds. This red panda was without the scars Jack had on his right eye, and he also looked much younger than Jack.

"Hey! What are you doing? Leave Doggy alone!" Flurry shouted. The bear cub ran over and stood between the red panda and Vallidore. Just then, Noah snuck up from behind, but got his legs swept out from under him by the red-furred visitor. The red panda was lightning fast. Before Noah could hit the ground, the red panda grabbed him by the arm and tossed him into Flurry and Drizzle, which knocked all three of them to the turf.

Flurry recovered quickly. He stood back up, but found the point of a sword directed at his nose. Noah got up and pushed Flurry back. The lanky lion stood between Flurry and the visitor's blade with his arms raised as a barrier to protect his friend.

"Stop!" murmured the white wolf. He had momentarily regained consciousness. "These are my friends. You must help us. Jack Frost did this." Vallidore then collapsed again.

The red panda put his sword back in the scabbard slung over his back. The red panda pulled out bandages from the pouch at his waist, and continued dressing Vallidore's wounds.

"I think he must be a friend," Drizzle told Flurry.

"Then why did he attack us?"

"He isn't now. He put his sword away. See! Maybe you should talk to him."

"Me? You talk to him!"

"Excuse me, sir. My name is Drizzle. That's Flurry, and the lion is Noah. We're looking for The Protectors. Would you be so kind as to tell us where they may be found? We need to find them so we can stop Jack."

"Oh, that won't be necessary!" came a bone-chilling voice in the distance. There stood Jack, alive and well. He confidently strolled toward them with his sword drawn. He wore a black leather trench coat which resembled a ship captain's jacket. "And who might you be?" he addressed the other red panda. "Serve me, and I'll let you live."

The small red panda stood up and readied his sword. The blade instantly glowed with a radiant blue light. The warrior pointed it at Jack. When Jack glimpsed the sword, he immediately recognized it. "That sword! I know that sword! That belonged to Tomodachi! You're one of Tomodachi's descendants, aren't you? I may not have had the pleasure of ending his life, but I can certainly end yours!"

With a wave of his free paw, Jack caused shards of ice to shoot through the air toward the other red panda, but the young warrior was too fast. He leapt out of the way and continued to do so time and time again with each successive wave.

To and fro the fellow dodged each blast of ice that Jack sent his way. He was a more formidable opponent than Vallidore was, and it was clear that he had been well versed in the secret martial art of Yujin Do.

The nimble little warrior swung at Jack. He missed the villain only by a hair. Their battle continued to escalate. Jack tried to use his powers over ice and cold to stop his rival, but the younger one always managed to dodge everything Jack sent his way.

Jack leapt into a large tree, and the other

warrior did likewise. Their blades clashed in fierce combat. The sound of metal striking metal resonated as they dueled among the branches.

"You're skilled! I'll give you that. You're certainly much better than that mutt over there!" Just then, the warrior sliced Jack across the left cheek. Jack was stunned for a moment. After the shock had passed, he shouted, "You just cut me, little one! Cutting me was a mistake!"

Jack's eyes burned with rage. He let out a war cry and locked blades again. This time Jack used his powers to send frost across his blade and to the blade of his opponent. If Jack's rival had not acted quickly, his sword would have been encased in ice. It might have even frozen the warrior along with it, but the young warrior's wits were as sharp as his blade. The warrior quickly detached a smaller blade, which had been interlocked with the main one. He let go of the main sword before the frost reached the hilt.

The warrior now pointed a smaller blade at Jack. Despite its inferior size, he knew how to wield it just as well as the larger one. They continued their battle for quite a while. Flurry, Drizzle, and Noah watched, helpless to do anything. Flurry occasionally tried to throw rocks at Jack, but the villain deflected them each time. "That worked once, you little brat, but it won't work a second time!" Jack shouted at Flurry.

Strangely, Jack was deeply perturbed by Flurry's presence. Their interactions took a toll on Jack for some unknown reason. Jack looked at Flurry and then back at the warrior. "I tire of this, and I have somewhere to be. We'll continue this later."

Jack jumped down from the tree and ran toward another tree that was much larger. Its proximity to Flurry was why Jack chose it. Flurry and Drizzle cringed as Jack drew near. A blue glowing sphere formed between his paws, and he cast the ball of frigid energy toward the tree. The towering piece of timber became frozen instantly. Jack swung his sword at the tree and sent it plummeting toward the cubs.

The mystery warrior leapt out from the branches of the tree and rushed to their rescue. The bear cubs were pushed out of the way by Noah. The red panda landed on the ground, ahead of the incoming tree, and struck it with his sword. The blade shattered the tree into numerous pieces. It looked like the tree had exploded after the warrior sliced through it.

The red panda looked up and found Jack absent from the scene. He was about to pursue the enemy, but Vallidore grabbed him by the tail. "Chingu, wait! Wait! Don't leave us! We need you! We all need to rest. Stay with us until morning, and then we can continue the hunt. I know of a way to catch up with him."

"Oh, so that's his name!" Flurry commented. "I was just going to call him 'friend'. Hello, Chingu. I'm Flurry!"

Chingu looked at Flurry and bowed. The three cubs bowed in return.

Meanwhile, back in Ursus, tension was high with war on the horizon. Christopher Kringle was completely attired in beautifully decorated battle armor and had a double-edged sword strapped to his back. His wife,

Catherine, stood by his side with her bow in hand and a quiver of arrows at her side.

They had positioned themselves at the southern route into Christopher's land. The couple waited in the cold for an assembly of horses to arrive with their riders.

As the warriors on horseback approached, Christopher put his arm around his wife's shoulder and waved with his free hand. One rider broke away from the company and rode out ahead of the others to greet the Kringles personally.

"Welcome!" Christopher addressed the man and bowed. The gentleman was very tall and slender. He wore silver armor with gold decoration upon it. His hair was long, straight, and blonde. In fact, the entire company of soldiers that came with him bore a striking resemblance. The most noticeable trait was that his ears came to a point.

The gentleman rode up to the Kringles. Christopher bowed again. "Prince Suladnia, I am in your debt."

"It's been a long time since we prepared for battle together. It's a shame that we have to meet under such dire circumstances," Suladnia answered.

"Indeed! We should catch up over dinner tonight. All of us need to be strong to win this battle," Christopher replied.

Suladnia revealed a hint of a smile from the corner of his mouth. The prince stepped down from his horse and approached Christopher. "That kind of thinking is going to make you fat, old friend; and if I remember correctly, you owe me dinner anyway."

They both laughed, reached out their right hands, and grasped each other at the wrist. "Welcome back!" Christopher replied.

"Thank you! It's good to be back," answered the prince.

"You remember Catherine."

"Indeed! My lady," Suladnia addressed her and bowed. "My men are in need of food and lodging. Is it too much to ask if …"

Before he could complete his sentence Christopher spoke up, "You don't ever need to ask a question like that. Preparations have been underway for quite some time. We're honored by your presence. Please follow us. We shall lead you and your company to your accommodations in Polaris. There you can rest and have some good food as well."

The elves trailed behind as the Kringles led the way to Polaris. The city of Polaris was much better suited for men than Ursus. Christopher had dominion over a very large region. Many people and animal groups in his land looked to him for protection and leadership.

Back at the forest, nightfall had caught up with the weary travelers. Vallidore snored throughout the night. The wolf finally acquired his much needed rest. Chingu and the cubs stayed up later than they should have, but Flurry and the others were infatuated with their new friend. Chingu turned out to not only be one of The Protectors, but he was THE Protector. He was the youngest of seven brothers, but had been deemed the most worthy to claim the sword of Tomodachi.

Tomodachi's sword had been passed down for many generations. The family heirloom was quite a marvelous-looking blade. It had two different parts that interlocked to become one larger sword which was sharp on both sides with an engraving on the blade. The part Flurry liked the most was that it glowed blue when pure evil was present – blue was Flurry's favorite color.

Eventually, the cubs grew sleepy enough to value their rest more than hearing stories. Soon they were fast asleep, and Chingu stood watch. He was a very devoted and faithful red panda. He always did what needed to be done, despite any cost to himself. Chingu valued honor and integrity above all else. He was also quite adept in his skills as a swordsman and master of Yujin Do, an ancient martial art named after Tomodachi the Great's daughter, Yujin.

Chingu was very sharp and alert at all times. Very little ever snuck by or fooled him. It was like he had a sixth sense. His own brothers believed that he had never slept a day in his life. They often joked that he was always on guard.

The morning came, and Flurry woke up to find food that had already been cooked and set on a plate beside him. While he slept, Chingu had gathered and prepared food for everyone. It was still very early, and the sun had barely crept over the horizon. Vallidore was awake and on his feet. His gaze was fixed on a clearing in the forest. Flurry was not aware of anything at first, because he was quite enamored with the food.

After he had finished his meal, Flurry noticed that Drizzle and Vallidore both stared in the direction of the clearing. Being the curious cub he was, Flurry squeezed between Vallidore and Drizzle. He pushed his way to the front to make sure he had the best view.

Down in the clearing, Flurry spotted Chingu and Noah. Flurry could not exactly make out what was going on, but it appeared that Chingu was teaching Noah the art of Yujin Do. Noah held a wooden staff and received instructions from Chingu about how to use it.

It was uncertain how much time had passed, but the sun had climbed considerably higher in the sky, and Vallidore was ready to continue his pursuit of Jack. Chingu and Noah returned to the camp, and Chingu walked up to speak privately with Vallidore. "You're right. I shall ask him," the white wolf replied to

Chingu.

Vallidore approached the cubs. "We've been discussing a strategy to deal with Jack, but we're sorely outnumbered. We know where Jack is going. He's on his way to Ursadoom, the impenetrable fortress of the polar bears. They're Jack's loyal subjects, and represent his strength at war. They've been hibernating for many years, but with Jack's return, they'll reawaken and attack the northern kingdoms without mercy. The only way we stand a chance is if we get help."

Vallidore looked right at Noah, "We need someone who can cross the desert to the city of Gargarin. Chingu has written instructions to be delivered to the king. There you may be able to find help that can get here quickly enough to stop Jack's attack before it begins.

Without this help, we'll certainly fail. Our numbers are too few. Even Chingu's brothers are too far off to be able to get here in time. Are you willing to do this, Noah?"

Noah stood up straight and nodded his head to indicate that he would do it. Noah's job was to protect Flurry. He had promised their mother. The best way to do this was to get help so that they could win the battle against Jack.

"The desert is very hot and treacherous, but we chose you because we believe you're the one who would most likely succeed, for you don't require food or drink. Who would've thought that not having a mouth would be such a great advantage?"

Noah saluted Vallidore and headed off in the direction that Chingu instructed him. With Noah on his way to find help, it left

Flurry and Drizzle to join Vallidore and Chingu. Together they rushed to Ursadoom to implement the second part of Chingu's plan.

What Flurry and Drizzle did not know was that they would have to travel through another forest that had a dark reputation. Kraeburne Forest was legendary for being a place of doom to anyone that entered, but it was a shortcut, and Vallidore believed they could catch up with Jack with this alternate route. The wolf believed that Jack would avoid the danger and take the long way around the forest. Little did Flurry know what was in store for them. They rode on Vallidore straight to the dark and foreboding forest. Kraeburne Forest housed creatures of pure shadow in physical form. It was a place of nightmares.

CHAPTER 6
KRAEBURNE FOREST

Fall leaned over the armrest of one of the Kringles' chairs and stared outside. It was close to midday, and she had decided to spend some time away from the rest of the teddy bear cubs. She occasionally needed time to herself to think things through, despite the fact she had done that very thing all evening long. She barely got any sleep the previous night. Fall had tossed and turned the night away with the same troubles she wrestled with now. The cub wondered where Flurry, Drizzle, and Noah were, what they might be doing, and if they were okay. She loved her brother very much, even if he frequently made her angry. She had also grown fond of her new friend Drizzle, and worried about how he and Flurry were getting along, if at all.

While she slouched over the armrest, she heard a commotion from the kitchen. Fall quickly jumped down and ran to investigate. When she entered the kitchen, she found Caboose on the floor with pots and pans all around him. He even had one on his head. "What are you doing?" Fall inquired. She was shocked that Caboose would be the cause of such a mess.

Before Caboose could answer, Boaz and Honja rushed in. "Oh no! This wouldn't have happened if you hadn't made me come back for you!" Boaz lectured the little rabbit. Honja crossed his arms and looked away. Boaz turned to Caboose. "Come on, Caboose! You've been at this all night long. I told you, Flurry isn't here!"

Fall giggled. "You mean Caboose is looking for Flurry?"

"Unfortunately, yes," Boaz answered after a long sigh.

Caboose got up and sniffed around the cabinets before he opened them up to peek inside. "Why is he looking for Flurry?"

"He thinks Flurry is playing hide-and-seek. I've told him countless times that we quit playing, but he doesn't believe me," Boaz explained.

"Caboose, Flurry went away," Fall told the little polar bear.

"He went away ... to hide," Caboose

replied. He was so sure of himself. "Oh! I know where he could be!" Caboose turned around and ran out of the room.

"Here we go again! Come on, Honja! Are you going to join us, Fall?" Boaz asked.

"Sure. Why not? It'll at least keep my mind occupied so I don't worry about my brother as much." Fall ran off with Boaz and Honja, in pursuit of their polar bear friend.

Unfortunately, Flurry was not having fun at all. He would have given anything to be back in Ursus with his friends. The forest was very dark and immensely creepy, even in the late afternoon.

"Doggy, why do we have to be in such a scary place?" Flurry spoke into Vallidore's ear.

"Speak softly. We're being watched," Vallidore replied.

Chingu jumped down from Vallidore's back and took point. He walked a few steps, raised his arm, and motioned for everyone to halt and be silent – and silent they were. In fact, the entire forest was still. No noise could be heard at all, not the rustling of leaves, the chirping of birds, nor even the whistle of the wind was present. If Flurry could describe it with one word, it would be "dead".

Flurry was grateful they were not there at night, but the sunlight did not diminish the terror he felt in such a place. None of the trees had any leaves. The branches were not only bare, but were also black instead of brown. The ground, blackened with mud, sported small patches of thorns which only grew in a few places. Beyond that, no other vegetation existed. The entire forest gave

Flurry a sense of dread and despair.

Chingu reached for his blade and pulled it from its scabbard. As Flurry expected, the blade glowed blue, which meant they were surrounded by something of pure evil. Flurry would have been more frightened if Vallidore had told him what lurked in the forest. The wolf did not want to disturb the cubs any more than they already were, but that was about to change.

Chingu believed they were about to be attacked by the shadow creatures. He simply knew them as the Kŭrimja. Their proper name was not known to him. Citizens of different nations each had a different name for these creatures of pure darkness. Chingu's mother had told him that they were called the Kŭrimja.

"You two, get down from my back and

take cover behind that stump in the path. We're about to be attacked," Vallidore softly commanded the cubs. "Chingu and I will protect you. They're only hurt by light. Unfortunately, the clouds are about to cover up the sun in a moment. Chingu has the most effective weapon to defend us with."

"But he only has one. He can't fight all of them," Flurry reasoned from the tree trunk he and Drizzle now hid behind.

Vallidore kept a sharp eye. He watched the shadows to see if any of them moved in a way that was not common for a true shadow. "Look out!" Vallidore shouted to Chingu.

The red panda glanced up and saw a large beast charge toward him with sharp teeth and razor-like claws. This was no ordinary beast; the creature was entirely made out of shadow.

Chingu swung his sword at his enemy. The creature took a leap back from him. Other creatures soon appeared and surrounded the group.

"I think coming here was a bad idea!" Drizzle shouted to Vallidore.

Vallidore growled and initiated his attack. He leapt at one of the creatures, gripped it with his mouth, and threw it down to the ground just as another one sprang onto his back and clawed at him. The white wolf howled in pain, but he continued to fight. Vallidore grabbed the creature by the head, threw it over his shoulders, and slammed it into a tree at the side of the path.

Meanwhile, Chingu was in a fierce battle of his own. He swung and stabbed at the various evil forms with a blade in each paw.

Some of them he wounded, while others ran to escape his blade but returned again to make a second attempt at his life.

At first, it appeared that Vallidore and Chingu might win, but then the ground rumbled. The trees swayed as something drew near. There were loud screeches, groans, roars, and growls that came from all around them. Flurry and Drizzle had been hiding, but Flurry peeked out from the tree stump and saw what it was. Terror came across the bear cub's face when he saw hundreds of shadow creatures that came from all directions.

The bear cubs continued to hide until Drizzle decided to try and help. He ran out into the battle and called to Chingu, "Give me your other sword!"

Chingu tossed the smaller blade to the

cub. Drizzle caught the glowing weapon and swung it at the creatures.

Flurry knew it would end badly for all of them. He had to think of a plan, and it had to be fast – besides, his pride would not allow Drizzle to get all of the glory for being a hero. "Think, Flurry! Think!" the bear whispered to himself. Then, in a moment of inspiration, Flurry had an idea. He raced out to the battle and took cover under Vallidore's legs. Vallidore swung at the creatures as their heated battle raged on. "Drizzle! I have an idea!"

"If you have an idea, we're doomed!" Drizzle replied.

"Hey! Stop that! I have an idea! I mean it!" Flurry answered.

Drizzle ran up, and Flurry told him the plan. "That's a terrible idea!" Drizzle adversely responded. "That could get you killed!" He was immensely concerned for Flurry's safety.

"Well, if you think it's a bad idea, that's all the more reason for me to do it," Flurry replied and darted up the path.

"Flurry, no! Stop!" Drizzle shouted.

Vallidore and Chingu looked, with horrified concern, when they saw Flurry race off on his own. "Flurry, stop! What are you doing? They'll come after you!" Vallidore shouted, but it was no use. Flurry was well on his way. He ran as fast as his little legs would take him. He never looked back, because he knew full well that he was being chased by the evil creatures from the darkness.

"Vallidore! Chingu! Hurry! Flurry is the decoy so we can escape the forest! Let's go!" Drizzle shouted.

"We can't just leave him!" Vallidore replied. "He's only a cub!"

"It's what he wanted! He's doing it so we can stop Jack! Stopping Jack is more important! We have to go! Now!"

Vallidore swallowed hard and fought back his tears. Chingu turned to them, nodded, and then leapt onto Vallidore's back. On his way up, Chingu pulled Drizzle onto Vallidore along with him. Before they had a chance to blink, Vallidore was off. He bolted through the forest as fast as he could. The trio attempted their escape while the creatures chased Flurry.

Flurry kept running. He knew that his sacrifice was necessary to save everyone he loved and cared about. Jack had to be stopped, and they would never catch up with

Jack if they could not make it out of the forest.

As Flurry ran, his mind raced. He thought about his parents and his sister. He also thought about his adopted family in Middleasia, and all of the new friends he had made. Flurry feared that he would never see any of them ever again. He worried that he might fail, and the next thing his parents would learn was that their son was no more. Tears streamed down his cheeks, but he kept running. Saving the lives of everyone else was more important than saving only himself. The creatures drew nearer. They howled, growled, and clawed at the bear cub.

Flurry ran to the edge of the forest at the top of a cliff. He had nowhere left to run. The clouds had become dark, as if a thunderstorm was coming. The shadow creatures surrounded him and clawed at him. If not for his plan, they would have ripped him apart, but Flurry was no fool. He reached into his coat pocket and pulled out the glowing gemstone he had taken from the cave. Flurry held it up above his head. The blue glow changed to pure white. The light radiated brighter and brighter. It was so intense that Flurry had to shield his eyes from it. A shockwave came forth from the crystal, which resulted in bloodcurdling screams. The creatures were all destroyed by the light.

Flurry opened his eyes. He looked around and saw scorch marks on the ground where the creatures once stood. Steam rose up from their black silhouettes. Flurry put the crystal back into his pocket and turned to head down the path, but he slipped and fell off the cliff. Luckily, the cliff was not too steep. He slid through black mud, down and down, until he came to a stop at the bottom of the slope. Flurry had arrived at the outer boundary of the forest.

He looked at his mud-covered clothes and sighed with frustration. "That figures. I save everyone, and then I have to be the one to get covered in mud. How am I going to get this mud out of my clothes?" Flurry muttered to himself.

"How about washing them?" came a familiar and welcome voice.

Flurry looked up and saw that Drizzle stood a few yards away with Vallidore and Chingu.

"Well done, my friend! Well done indeed!" praised Vallidore.

Chingu simply nodded in approval. Drizzle ran up and helped Flurry to his feet. "You know, even though it worked, it was still a pretty bad idea." Drizzle winked.

Flurry smiled and rejoined his friends. They all climbed up onto Vallidore's back, and away they went. They were very near to Ursadoom, and Vallidore was making good time. It would not be long before they arrived.

Noah, on the other hand, was still traveling a seemingly never-ending path. The sun was hot, and its rays beat down on him. The intense heat rose up from the sand. Noah thought it looked like oil, from a distance. Despite how hot it was, Noah had the advantage of being a plush lion. He had no need for food or water, and he did not sweat.

He held the wood staff tightly in his paw. The lion pushed forward throughout the day and into the early evening. The sun had reached the horizon when he spotted something large up ahead. At last! Noah could see a magnificent city in the distance. He pressed on with renewed vigor. He had made it! Before long, Noah approached the walled-in city of massive proportions. A palace sat on a hill at the center of the stone metropolis.

Noah wanted to ensure Flurry's safety and be able to keep his promise to their mother. He would never be able to face her again if anything happened to Flurry. He would have been frantic had he known what Flurry did in Kraeburne forest. Luckily, he was not there to witness the horrors of that place.

Noah reached the outer walls of the city, where two very large lion-like creatures stood guard. Though they resembled lions, they were much larger, and their bodies were covered with armor plating. They also had bumps and horns that protruded from their heads in various places. They did not speak to Noah, nor did they acknowledge his presence in any way. The gates to Gargarin were wide open for anyone to come or go as they pleased.

After he entered the city, Noah saw a vast marketplace with vendors of every kind. It was quite diverse, with different types of animals and people. He saw dwarves, elves, and humans in the mix with creatures he did not recognize.

Noah pushed through the crowds of merchants and consumers, and shifted his gaze up at the palace. He knew he would have to go there and meet with the king. Noah set off toward the king's hill as swiftly as he could, for he had important business to take care of.

Nightfall had come. Flurry and Drizzle stood at a distance with Vallidore and Chingu. They peered down at the fortress of Ursadoom. The air was so cold and crisp that they could see their own breath.

"We're here," Vallidore informed his companions. "Unfortunately, I believe we're too late. The polar bears are awake and are prepared for battle. This calls for a change in plans."

Vallidore and Chingu walked off a short distance to discuss strategy. Drizzle shivered a few feet away from Flurry. Flurry felt fine; the cold never bothered him. He only wore the winter coat because his father made him do it. Despite Flurry's opinion, the region was quite cold. In fact, the land looked like a solid piece of cracked ice. The ground was completely barren. The only feature to the landscape was that of the fortress which overlooked a cliff down into a canyon. It was a long way down if anyone were to topple over the side.

Vallidore returned. "We have to stall them."

"How are we going to do that?" Flurry asked in a tone of disbelief.

"Yeah! We can't even get into the fortress," Drizzle added.

"I believe there's a way in. Chingu mentioned that Jack has a strong negative reaction to you." Vallidore looked right at Flurry as he spoke.

"Me?" Flurry replied.

"Yes, you. Why is this?"

"How should I know?"

"Well, I believe that if you try to get his attention, he won't be able to resist coming out to get you. When he opens the gate, Chingu and Drizzle will sneak inside. They'll let me in later, at the appropriate time."

"Oh no! I'm not doing that! Jack will kill me!"

"We'll be there to protect you," Vallidore tried to assure the teddy bear cub.

"Fine, but I don't like this plan!" Flurry replied begrudgingly.

After going over their plans in great detail, Flurry was ready to go. He hustled down the slope and across the frozen plain. As Flurry stood outside the main gate, he realized that he had not even been detected by the guard posts up high on the fortress walls. "Man! They must really be busy to not see me," Flurry said to himself.

Flurry looked around and saw Drizzle and Chingu, one on each side of the castle entrance. They were both spread flat against the wall and ready to sneak in when the gate opened. Vallidore watched from a distance but was ready in case anything went wrong.

"Hello?" Flurry shouted. He could hear his own voice echo. "Hello?" he called out again. He waited, but still no reply. Flurry decided to shout louder. "Hey! I'm talking to you!" Still nothing but silence.

Flurry paced back and forth. He looked at the frozen ground and kicked at the snow. He wondered what he would have to do to get someone's attention. Flurry played with his coat pockets to pass the time. He was too bored to stop fiddling around with them. The little cub opened and closed each pocket over and over.

From the castle lookout, a polar bear guard, in his Roman-like armor, saw a light from afar. It came from the crystal in Flurry's pocket. It acted like a strobe light going on and off, as Flurry kept opening and closing his pocket. The polar bear guard summoned his master. Jack came to the lookout. "What is it? This had better be good!"

"What's that?" asked the bear. He pointed to the bright flashing light in the distance.

Jack looked out over the wall but could not make out what the pulsating light source in the distance was. He was about to ignore it when he heard humming. "That voice! I know that voice!" Jack ran back up to the wall and shouted down from above. "Who goes there? It better not be who I think it is!"

"Oh, hi, Mr. Meanie Pants! It's me, Flurry!"

Jack was instantly an emotional wreck. There was something about Flurry that got under his skin. "You! I still haven't rid myself of you yet?"

"Nope!" Flurry answered.

"Away with you! I'll deal with you later! I have a kingdom to conquer tomorrow. If you're lucky, maybe you can be among the slain."

"Looks to me like you're hiding."

"I'm not hiding!"

"Yes, you are!"

"No, I'm not!"

"You're the one in a fortress, not me."

"Be quiet!"

"No, you be quiet!"

"Ahhh! I've heard enough!"

"You just don't like it that I'm so cute, and you're not. Hee, hee, hee, hee, hee."

Jack shook with rage. Flurry's giggle was the last straw for him. He could not take it anymore. "That's it! I have an opening in my schedule! I guess there's always room to destroy you!" Jack stormed off and shouted an order to his polar bear followers. "Someone go get that pest, and throw him in the dungeon! I'll deal with him in the morning!"

The gate opened. Nearly a dozen polar bear warriors rushed toward him, decked out in their shiny armor. Flurry felt proud. He had accomplished his part in the plan. When the polar bears were about to seize him,

Drizzle and Chingu slipped into the fortress undetected. Vallidore was pleased with what he witnessed from the ridge. Their plans were off to a good start. Now it was time for phase three.

CHAPTER 7
THE BATTLE AT URSADOOM

Morning came, but it brought another overcast day. The sun could not be seen, and the cold wind whistled through the windows. Fall sat up and shivered at the sound. She pulled her blanket aside, got down from the bed, and went out into the main hall. She had spent the past night with the other bear cubs in the same room they had all been in since the night of the storm. It was hard to believe that this was the third morning since she and Flurry came to Mr.

and Mrs. Kringle's house.

A tear dropped from her eye as she thought about her brother. She probably would have broken down and cried if she had not been distracted by the noise outside. Fall ran up to the nearest window and peered out at the company of warriors, both humans and elves, gathered together.

"What's going on?" asked Boaz, as he came out of the room and rubbed his eyes. He had been roused from his sleep by all of the chatter beyond the walls of the hall.

"I don't know, but I see many men in armor, carrying weapons," Fall answered. "I think I see Mrs. Kringle! She's carrying a bow. She has a dagger, and arrows strapped to her waist, too. I wonder what's going on."

"Whatever it is, it can't be good," Boaz replied.

"She's coming! Quick! Act normal!" Fall and Boaz ran to the middle of the room, and pretended like they had been playing with a deck of cards when the lady entered.

Catherine called for all of her house guests to join her in the main hall. After everyone was awake and gathered together, she made her announcement. "Everyone! Listen up! My scouts have reported that Jack and his polar bear army are preparing for battle at this very moment. I won't lie to you; it's highly probable that we're going to be under attack soon. Our home will be a prime target. You'll not be safe here. So gather only what you can carry. My husband and I will be leading two separate battle groups soon. We need to relocate all of you now." Catherine's voice was stern, and her words were taken seriously. Everyone jumped up, gathered their things, and followed her out of the set of double doors.

"Wait! Where's Caboose?" Fall asked Boaz.

"I have no idea. I gave up on him yesterday," Boaz replied.

"Oh no! I hope he's okay."

"I'm sure he's fine. Let's go!"

Boaz, Honja, and Fall walked out together, and the doors were closed and locked behind them. The house was now empty and silent, except for the faint sound of footsteps that could be heard from the main stairway. Caboose was still on the search for Flurry. He arrived at the banquet hall and saw that it was empty. "Oh! So everyone's hiding again! Okay, here I come, ready or not!" Caboose diligently looked under couches and inside drawers.

Daylight entered through the open window of the dungeon where Flurry had been locked up. It was very small and unpleasant. The room was without a bed, blanket, or comfort of any kind. Flurry sat in his cold, damp cell and tried to think of a way to escape. While he plotted, his thoughts were interrupted by the creak of the dungeon door being opened. Two polar bear soldiers came down the steps, followed by the evil red panda himself. Jack held Flurry's crystal in his paw.

"Well, now that I've had a wonderful night's sleep, it's time to deal with you. I want to be sure that I've rid myself of you before going into battle. It's good for morale." Jack snickered. "Oh! I must thank you for handing this over to me." Jack held up the crystal, but for some reason it did not glow. It looked like an ordinary stone in Jack's grip. "I'm not sure how you got this without being turned into ice, but it clearly has power that I can utilize for my own purposes. So, tell me. How does it work?"

"It won't do you any good. It only works for me," Flurry answered.

"Really? What makes you think that?" Jack skeptically replied.

"Uh … I don't know. Just a guess."

"No matter! I'll find a way to use it, and if not, it's no loss to me. I don't fuss over spilled milk. The important thing is that I'll finally be rid of you, after all of these years." Jack placed the crystal down on a table and approached Flurry's cell. "Now, where were we? Ah yes! I believe I was about to have you ripped from limb to limb." Jack clapped his paws and shouted,

"Guards!"

Flurry was confused about how or why Jack acted like he knew him. That simply could not be possible. In the middle of his thought, the polar bears came toward Flurry's cell, unlocked it, and dragged him out.

"Let go of me! Put me down!" Flurry shouted and struggled against the strength of the brutes.

"Ha, ha, ha, ha, ha. I don't think so!" Jack replied, amused that Flurry would expect them to comply.

"If you don't let me go, you'll be sorry!"

"The only thing I'm sorry about is that I didn't do this sooner."

"Chingu, would you like to help me out?"

Jack was startled by Flurry's statement. He spun around and beheld Chingu as he descended the steps toward the villain. The young warrior approached. He looked calm and sure of himself.

"Get him!" Jack ordered the guards.

"But what about this one?" they inquired about Flurry.

"Throw him back in his cell!" Jack shouted. After the guards tossed Flurry back, Jack pushed the two bears out ahead of himself to confront Chingu on his behalf.

Chingu was truly a magnificent warrior. He drew his sword and quickly dispensed with the henchmen.

"What good is having an army if they can't fight?" Jack muttered to himself. He drew his sword and sprinted up the steps at Chingu. As Jack came near, Chingu's sword glowed its radiant blue.

Jack shouted, "Fine! I'll do this myself!"

Their swords crossed. The clanging of their blades echoed throughout the stone walls of the dungeon. Their duel led them up the steps and out onto the battlements.

Flurry tried to find a way out of his cell, but it was no use. He was locked up tight and wondered if he would ever get out. Flurry heard someone enter the dungeon. They approached the door to his cell. Flurry listened to the sound of his cell's lock being manipulated. The door swung open. Drizzle stood there with a smug look on his face. "Yep! I figured out that puzzle lock all by myself. You're welcome!" Drizzle informed the freed captive.

"Yeah, yeah, whatever! We have to get out of here! Let's go!" Flurry replied, dashed over to the table, and grabbed the gemstone. It instantly lit back up again.

Flurry shoved it down into his coat pocket and ran up the steps with Drizzle. When they exited the dungeon, they noticed that Jack and Chingu continued to battle with each other while Jack's army stood down below and spectated.

"Now's our chance!" Drizzle shouted. He grabbed Flurry by the arm and led him down the steps to the main gate. "We have to get this gate open so we can let Vallidore in. Give me a hand."

"You mean paw?" Flurry sarcastically replied.

"Not now, Flurry! You know what I mean!" Drizzle answered.

Flurry and Drizzle pushed as hard as they could on the lever which would activate the gate. The mechanism that worked the gate ran on a series of weights and pulleys. The lever activated a winch that would raise the gate on its own. It was no use; the cubs simply did not have the strength to do the job. They continued to try. Flurry and Drizzle both pushed on the release lever, but they were unable to make it budge even an inch.

They panted and grunted. Before they could make another attempt, one of the polar bears glanced in their direction and spotted them. He shouted, "You two! Hold it right there!" The ferocious bear bustled toward them. The beast roared and attempted to snatch them in his mouth, but missed. The cubs jumped down and darted in opposite directions.

Flurry was inspired. He ran back over to the lever and climbed up on it. The cub taunted the bear. "You're too slow! I bet you can't catch me!"

The burly bear leapt at Flurry, but the cub had the enemy right where he wanted him. Flurry jumped away from the lever, and the polar bear struck it with his head. The collision released the lever, and caused the gate to open.

"Yay!" the cubs shouted in unison. Jack heard their voices, and turned to look down at them. Chingu took advantage of the opportunity and struck Jack right in the jaw with the handle of his sword. It looked like Chingu might win, but Flurry and Drizzle were in big trouble. The other polar bears glared right at them, and immediately sped toward them. Flurry and Drizzle made a hasty retreat, but they were cut off and surrounded by Jack's army.

Fear overtook Flurry and Drizzle. Their

legs shook with terror. A polar bear opened his mouth wide and proceeded to chomp down on Flurry. As the bear's teeth began to close, Flurry saw his life flash before his eyes. Then something happened that nobody foresaw. Another animal with golden fur jumped into the polar bear's mouth, and lodged a wooden staff between its teeth. The bear was unable to close his mouth. The guard frantically tried to remove the staff and staggered off in pain.

"Noah!" Flurry shouted.

The lion cub had come to the rescue! The other polar bears were about to attack when suddenly the castle was overrun by hundreds of lion-like creatures in battle armor. A massive skirmish broke forth. Flurry and Drizzle took cover with Noah behind nearby crates.

Vallidore and the warriors from Gargarin engaged in a ferocious battle with the polar bears. It was unlike anything Flurry or his friends had ever seen before. The Gargarins and the polar bears struck, bit, and threw each other around as they each struggled for supremacy over the other.

The battle was going well on the ground, but not so for Chingu. Jack was now winning the duel. "Look!" shouted Drizzle. He pointed up at Jack. Flurry and Noah gazed up as Jack struck Chingu in the face.

"No!" Drizzle shouted. "We have to do something!"

"What can we do?" Flurry asked. The cub looked to Noah and Drizzle for answers. Noah shrugged, but Drizzle calculated something in his head.

Jack and Chingu continued their struggle

against each other, but Chingu was badly wounded. Jack repeatedly struck the weakened warrior. Chingu was almost out of strength. In a moment of desperation, Chingu separated his blades and fought with both at the same time. Jack laughed and knocked the blades out of Chingu's weakened paws.

"Thousands of years have passed, and this is the best Tomodachi's bloodline has to offer? You aren't half the warrior he was, and even he was no match for me. So what made you think that you could beat me?" Jack pushed Chingu down and jumped onto his victim's chest. It was clear that Jack was about to deliver the finishing blow.

Flurry was horrified. "We have to do something now!"

"Go distract him! I have a plan!" Drizzle

commanded.

"Don't do anything foolish!" Flurry insisted.

"I'm sure you'll think my plan is foolish, but if you'd think it's a foolish idea, that's all the more reason for me to do it!"

"Hey! You stole that phrase from me!"

"Go already!" Drizzle dashed up the steps and out onto the battlements. His plan was risky, but he could not let anything happen to his first true friend.

Flurry ran out into the heated battle between the polar bears and Gargarin warriors. One polar bear leapt for Flurry, but Noah jumped into the air and struck the polar bear in the face. It was enough to stun the guard while a Gargarin knocked him to the ground. "Wow!" Flurry was enamored by Noah. The lion cub simply pointed up at

Chingu to get Flurry to focus.

"Hey! Jack! You must not be that great! You still haven't beaten me yet, and I'm just a little cub!" Flurry shouted up at the villain.

Normally, Jack might not have heard someone shout from within such a loud battle, but his ears were tuned to Flurry's voice. When he heard the cub speak it acted like fingernails on a chalkboard to him. Jack quickly turned and stared at Flurry with rage in his eyes.

"I'm coming for you next! First, you can watch your friend die!" Jack raised the sword above his head with the tip pointed down at Chingu. He was about to stab The Protector when something completely unexpected happened. It was as if time had slowed to a crawl. What unfolded put a look of horror upon Flurry and Noah's faces.

Before Jack could deliver his death-dealing strike, Drizzle rushed across the battlements. The cub yelled, "Leave my friend alone!" and tackled Jack. Drizzle's high speed collision knocked both of them over the side of the wall.

"Drizzle! Nooo!" Flurry rushed up the steps and to the side of the wall. The cub peered over and faintly saw Jack and Drizzle fall to their doom in the canyon below. Flurry dropped to the stone floor and mourned. "No! How could this happen? He's gone!" Flurry buried his face in his paws and cried harder than he had ever cried. Noah came to Flurry's side and put his arm around him. Noah's face streamed with tears of his own.

The polar bear army stood still, as if they had become statues of ice. They could not believe that their leader was dead. Jack's death had taken the fight out of them all. They were now without a purpose or a leader to rally behind. The polar bears each laid down their arms and surrendered to the Gargarin warriors. The day had been won!

The Gargarins roared in victory, and Vallidore howled. Chingu slowly sat up and rubbed his head. Noah rushed to his side and helped him to his feet. Everyone down below cheered, but Chingu did not join in the merriment. Instead, he peered over the wall. Tears came to his eyes as he searched for any sign of life, but none was found.

They had saved everyone from the evil Jack Frost, but at a very high price. For Flurry, that cost was too unbearable to even think about. He and Drizzle had not always gotten along, but he had grown to respect him. No matter how bad their interactions were, Flurry never would have wished something so horrible on anyone, especially not on Drizzle.

Flurry remained on the stone surface of the battlements and cried. A great deal of time passed. Vallidore and the company of Gargarin warriors secured Ursadoom. They put the polar bears down in the dungeon, and sent out heralds to inform the surrounding regions of Jack's defeat.

Noah and Chingu helped Flurry to his feet and walked him down the steps where Vallidore waited. They placed Flurry on the white wolf's back, and Noah climbed up after him. Chingu refused to leave with them and stood by while they exited the gate of Ursadoom.

As they rode away, Flurry asked, "Why

isn't Chingu coming with us?"

"He'll not rest until he finds Drizzle's body. He has vowed to find it and bring it back to Ursus for a proper burial. He believes Drizzle deserves a hero's ceremony," Vallidore answered.

The wolf's explanation only brought more pain to Flurry's delicate little heart. He continued to cry, and buried his face in Vallidore's fur. They rode across the plain together. Ursus was their next destination. It was a bright day for all of the lands when they heard of Jack's defeat – it was a bright day for most, but not all. All of the different nations celebrated. Nobody ever had to fear Jack's tyranny ever again.

Vallidore arrived in Ursus early the next morning and found a massive crowd that had waited for their return. There were men, elves, and teddy bears all gathered together. Confetti rained down from above, and everyone cheered at their arrival. The weather had also changed. It was much warmer, and the sun had come out. It was a gorgeous day, but Flurry was unable to enjoy any of it.

As they approached, Christopher Kringle came forward and dismounted Flurry and Noah from Vallidore's back. "Welcome home! You two have made me proud. Everyone can live in peace, because of your bravery and sacrifice."

"It wasn't us. It was Drizzle who saved everyone. He made the real sacrifice." Flurry spoke quietly. He held his gaze at the snow-covered ground and rubbed tears from his eyes.

Christopher's face was filled with

empathy and grief of his own when he realized that Drizzle was not with them. "Indeed! He was a true hero, and he won't be forgotten," Christopher answered. The man stood back up. He clapped his hands, and servants came forth to attend to Flurry, Noah, and Vallidore's needs.

The melancholy mood was palpable. Kringle himself looked downcast. The villagers had no idea what to say or how to comfort the cubs. It was a bittersweet experience to be rid of Jack, but to lose Drizzle, too.

Later that day, a memorial service was held for the fallen cub. Honor was given to the brave and courageous bear who had sacrificed everything to save his friends and family from the cruelty and suffering that Jack would have brought upon the land.

Flurry, Fall, and Noah showed the most anguish. They had come to know Drizzle on a whole new level. They had grown to really love and respect him. Flurry looked around for Drizzle's parents, but they were not present for the service. Flurry felt a tremendous amount of grief for Drizzle's sake. He felt that someone should speak on Drizzle's behalf if his own family would not be there to do it.

Flurry stepped forward, wiped his tears, and cleared his throat. "I hardly knew him. We didn't get along. I thought he was weird. He talked forever about stuff that was boring to me. I didn't try to know him. Now I wish I had tried harder. He was a really great bear, and he was brave." Flurry's tears flowed profusely. "If not for Drizzle, we might not be alive. I'll miss him. He was my friend."

The crowd cried at the cub's heartfelt words. Mourners left flowers on the memorial stone. Fall had her arms around her brother while he wept.

Evening came, despite the sun having held its place in the arctic sky. It had been many hours since the memorial service. Flurry sat in one of Christopher's chairs and stared blankly out the window. "Come on! Let's go play!" Fall insisted after she rushed up to her brother and slugged him on the arm.

"I don't feel like it," Flurry moped.

"Flurry, I'm sad, too, but we can't dwell on that right now. Come on! It'll take your mind off of Drizzle for a bit. You should be so proud of what you accomplished. Thanks to you, I was freed from one of Jack's traps in the cave. Then you …"

"Drizzle did it," Fall's words were cut short by Flurry's succinct response.

"What? What do you mean?"

"Drizzle freed you. I only made things worse. If not for him, you would've died. It's my fault that you almost died." Flurry refused to make eye contact. "I wish Drizzle were here." The cub cried and rubbed his eyes.

Fall was shocked by the revelation. She had not realized it was Drizzle who saved her life. She assumed Flurry had freed her from the room she had been trapped in. Fall had not even been able to thank Drizzle. Tears filled her eyes. She joined Flurry and cast a blank stare out the window, before she turned and shuffled away, grief stricken.

She had not gone far when Noah rushed

into the room. He ran up to Flurry, tugged on his arm, and pointed at the window.

"What is it, Noah? I'm not in the mood," Flurry answered.

Noah pulled out a pad of paper and wrote, "Look!"

Fall read it and glanced outside. "Someone's coming!" she shouted.

Fall ran over and yanked on Flurry's other arm. Flurry felt annoyed. He sighed and alighted from the chair to approach the door. The door opened a moment before they arrived with Flurry. Christopher Kringle stood at the threshold.

"Ah! Just the three I was looking for. Come with me!" Christopher instructed them.

They stepped outside. Flurry shielded his eyes from the bright sun. At a distance stood two figures. Flurry's eyes adjusted and saw one of them was Chingu. A moment later, Flurry was able to make out the form of the other. The other individual had black fur and a red scarf.

Flurry's eyes widened, and a joyous smile came to his face. "Drizzle!" Flurry shouted. He ran up and hugged his friend.

Fall jumped up and down and clapped. She ran over and joined her brother and Drizzle for a group hug.

"How's this possible?" Flurry asked. "I saw you fall! I thought you were dead!"

"I did fall, but I survived somehow. I only remember falling, and then I woke up and saw Chingu kneeling over me. I might not have made it back here alive if not for Chingu, though. He found me laying in a tree along the bank of the river; he took care of me and protected me all the way back home," Drizzle answered.

Chingu approached the cubs. He drew his sword, detached the smaller blade, and handed it to Drizzle. A tear came to Drizzle's eye. "I can't accept this," he said. Drizzle tried to hand it back to the red panda. Chingu held Drizzle's paws closed, over the blade, and pushed Drizzle's arms back toward the cub's chest so that he knew it was a gift that he could keep.

"Friend," Chingu said, and then bowed to Drizzle.

Drizzle was speechless. He had no idea what to say, for his dream had come true. He now had a true friend. With teary eyes, Drizzle bowed in return.

Chingu also bowed to everyone else before he turned and walked off toward the arctic sun. "Do you think we'll ever see him again?" asked Flurry. He looked up at Christopher for an answer.

The man chuckled, "I'm certain of it! Now come! We have a celebration to attend!" The cubs all went with Christopher back into the house.

Caboose ran out and shouted, "Sare you are! I found you! I win!"

"Huh?" Flurry looked to anyone that could give him an answer.

"It's a long story. It's better not to ask," Fall replied.

Boaz and Honja ran into the room behind Caboose. Flurry was happy to see them again. They all exchanged greetings, hugged, and enjoyed their night together. Everyone was happy. Mr. and Mrs. Snow were so proud of their son and daughter.

They smiled and watched their cubs play and giggle together.

They all laughed and ate the night away. The following morning came far too quickly. Flurry stood in his parents' bathroom. He brushed his fur and straightened his scarf. The cub had to look good before he returned home to Middleasia. Luckily, Christopher informed Flurry's human mother that he had extended Flurry's stay, so she would not be worried about his absence. Flurry was only supposed to be gone for a few days, not a couple of weeks.

"Flurry! It's time to go!" shouted Mrs. Snow, from the first floor.

Flurry ran out of the room and found Fall in the hallway. She stood there with her arms extended. "You're not going without a hug," she said.

Fall gave Flurry the warmest hug a sister could give to her brother and accompanied him down the steps. Flurry, Fall, Noah, Caboose, Boaz, and Honja all left with Mr. and Mrs. Snow. They walked to the town center together. In the middle of the plaza, Mr. and Mrs. Kringle, Vallidore, and Drizzle stood by and waited for their arrival.

"Goodbye! I'm actually going to miss you," Drizzle told Flurry.

"Yeah, I think I'll miss you, too," Flurry answered and gave Drizzle a hug. "I guess that makes us friends."

They all exchanged farewells and were about to embark on their trip home, when Christopher called out, "Not so fast! I have something for you."

"Oooh! A gift? What is it? Is it cookies?"

Flurry was so excited.

Christopher chuckled. "No, but it's something very special. This gift has been in your family for thousands of years. I've been watching over it for safe keeping. When I saw what you did during your visit, I was reassured that its proper keeper should be you. So here you go. Keep it safe. Don't open it until you get home. Okay?"

"Yes, Santa!" Flurry answered and quickly snatched the package away to hug it in his arms. Flurry led the cubs out of town. Flurry's brothers from Middleasia all trailed behind him in their little caravan.

They turned the corner to go down the next street. Drizzle ran after them to say one last goodbye, but they were no longer there. It was as if they had vanished into thin air. Drizzle waved his arm and softly whispered,

"Goodbye."

Back in Middleasia, Flurry's mother and father sat on the couch and watched a movie together. There was a knock at the door. Flurry's daddy got up and went to investigate. He peeked through the peephole, but did not see anyone there. "That's weird," he said.

He stuck his head out from the door to look around. As soon as it opened, five balls of fur rushed into the house and shouted, "Mommy! Daddy! We're home!"

The couple was overjoyed. All five brothers jumped on their mother's lap and hugged her. It was a wonderfully delightful day, and Flurry was glad to finally be back home.

EPILOGUE
THE END?

The sound of a thunderous waterfall echoed throughout a lush, green valley. The air was humid, and the temperature was searing hot. River water rushed quickly past the sandy banks. Water poured out over a massive stone monument of a decorative figure. Below the chiseled monolith lay an animal on the shore. It had red fur, a striped tail, and wore a black ship captain's trench coat.

A cloaked figure approached from the tree line and rolled the red panda over onto his back.

The red panda was weak and near death. He opened his eyes and coughed, "Where am I?"

"Shhhhh!" said the cloaked female. "Don't speak! You're very seriously wounded. Your injuries are fatal. You'll probably not live much longer."

"Help me!" Jack tried to command her, but his voice was hoarse.

"You're near death, but I know someone who can help you. However, the healing method won't be pleasant. It'll be an intensely painful process for you. You'll live … for a price," answered the mysterious female.

"Do it," Jack murmured in his weakened and nearly lifeless state.

"Are you sure?"

"Do it!" came his weary attempt to yell at her.

"Very well," she replied and removed her hood, which revealed her to be a koala bear. She shouted back toward the waterfall, "Bring him in! We have a life to save."

A tall, pale snow leopard approached. He wore a purple robe adorned with decorative gold markings. The cat knelt down next to Jack. "Are you ready?" Jack nodded his head. The snow leopard replied, "Very well then, let's begin!"

*****

Back in Middleasia, Flurry pondered the events of the previous weeks. He had learned a priceless lesson on his adventure. He realized that everyone was important, and no matter how strange or different someone seemed to be, they always had something of value to offer.

Now, one could not help but wonder what happened with Drizzle. Could Drizzle have really survived such a plunge into the depths of the canyon, when Jack himself was near death? Flurry had wished to see Drizzle again – and as we all know, Flurry had a special ability to make his wishes come true. So was it just luck that Drizzle lived, or did Flurry have anything to do with it?

In all of the excitement of Flurry's return to Middleasia, he had yet to open the package Christopher sent back with him. In fact, two months passed with the package tucked away under his bed. Flurry had been so busy playing and having fun with his friends that he had forgotten about it.

One night, Flurry lay in bed unable to sleep. He got up to make a gift for his mother when he realized that the unopened package sat below his bedframe. He dove under his bed and dug around for the parcel.

"What are you up to now?" Boaz grumbled.

"Oh my! I can't believe that I forgot about Santa's gift!" Flurry exclaimed from the darkness in his corner of the room.

Flurry pulled the package out and ripped the paper off to reveal an old, dusty book with a locked clasp. The hardbound text had decorative metals and precious stones laid into its cover. Most peculiarly, the center of the cover had an indentation that was empty. It appeared to Flurry that something belonged there, but it had been taken out.

A folded slip of paper stuck out from the

book's pages. Flurry removed it and opened it up, but he was unable to read it. He handed it to Boaz, who was now out of bed and had come to Flurry's side.

"What does it say?" Flurry asked.

Boaz put on his glasses. "This side says, *The Book of Snow*," he answered. The lion cub flipped the folded paper open and read aloud: "I believe this belongs to you. Signed, C.K."

"Hmmm." Flurry was very curious. Just at that moment a glow came from the drawer of his nightstand. Flurry got up, opened the drawer, and grabbed the crystal he had stashed away there. It shone brightly. Right before their eyes, the beautiful gem changed shape in Flurry's paw.

"Look! It's the size of that hole in the book!" exclaimed Boaz. The lion directed

Flurry's attention to the book's cover.

Being curious, Flurry placed the stone into the open hole. Immediately the book's clasp unhinged, and it sprang open. Blue light beamed out from the pages of the book. Flurry reached out and turned a page. This began Flurry's next great adventure.

ABOUT J.S. SKYE

J.S. Skye grew up in the Midwestern region of the United States. At a very young age, it was apparent that he was very talented. Finding that he was gifted in music and art, he plunged himself into both. As time passed, he set aside music to focus even more of his attention on developing his skills as an illustrator.

All throughout his years in school, J.S. Skye spent every available moment creating and developing fictional worlds. Caring about realism, he developed multiple people groups, countries, worlds, and even languages. His fictional realms were created through both written and visual mediums.

After traveling to almost a dozen different countries and studying different cultures, J.S. Skye decided to implement his interests in ancient cultures, history, languages, mythology, and more into his writings. He decided it was best to pour his heart and passion into writing instead of having divided interests between both art and literature.

J.S. Skye has accumulated a fairly large collection of his various writings. These stories range from all types of different genres such as mystery, science fiction, fantasy, and even horror. Friends encouraged the aspiring writer to produce a novel and see how things progressed from there.

J.S. Skye's first novel, *The Granted Wish*, was met with cheerful affirmation. The positive feedback was overwhelming and unexpected. Fans of his *Flurry the Bear* novels grew and began to clamor for more. From this point forward, his first novel series came to be.

For more information or to get in touch with J.S. Skye personally, he may be contacted by e-mail at:

JS-Skye@FlurryTheBear.com

ALSO BY J.S. SKYE

Flurry the Bear – The Granted Wish

Flurry the Bear – The Land of the Sourpie

Flurry the Bear – The Book of Snow

Flurry the Bear – The Rising Tide

www.ingramcontent.com/pod-product-compliance
Lightning Source LLC
Chambersburg PA
CBHW030306180626
46810CB00003B/939